G.A. EVERETT

HUNTED

DISCONNECTED
SERIES PREQUEL

HUNTED

DISCONNECTED SERIES PREQUEL

G. A. EVERETT

EVERETT OSTRICHES PUBLISHING

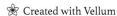 Created with Vellum

THANK YOU

Huzzah! You have stumbled upon my novel. This makes YOU the person I lay awake at night thinking about, dreaming, hoping would someday pick up a copy of one of my novels and dive willingly into its world.

If you do enjoy my work, and you fancy following along with what I'm up to, you can listen to my podcast *The G. A. Everett Story Club* over on Patreon.com/gaeverett, where I also provide book and film recommendations every month. You can also visit my website gaeverett.com to sign up to my newsletter.

You may have come to this novel because you chanced upon it, you liked the cover, the premise, or even because somebody recommended it to you (one can dream). Reading, for me, was always a thoroughly enjoyable pastime, along with music, film and theatre, in which I could escape from my everyday life to go on adventures, uncover crimes, slay dragons, or fall in love, if just for a moment. Whatever your reason for choosing my novel, I hope you enjoy reading it as much as I did writing it.

Happy reading.

NOVELS BY G. A. EVERETT

Hunted (Disconnected series prequel)

Artificial (Disconnected #1)

1

'**I** spy with my little eye, something beginning with G,'
Zaheera said.

'Goggles?' Johnson guessed, tapping the visor on his helmet.

'Nope.' Zaheera undid the lid of her water bottle and emptied its contents into her parched throat. The water was boiling. *Everything* was boiling here. The heat was as unbearable today as every other day she had spent in Helmand province in the last three months. She looked out of the small rectangular slit that passed for a window of the fifteen-ton armoured security vehicle and checked either side of the dirt road.

So far, so good.

'Glock?' Johnson asked, this time tapping the pistol currently secured to his side.

'Nope. Give up?'

'Never. Give us a clue, Major.'

'Yeah, inside or outside?' Rodriguez chimed in.

Zaheera made a pretence of scanning the convoy ahead. 'That's a tough one to answer. For the sake of you two morons, let's say inside. And you,' she looked at Rodriguez, 'you keep your hands on the wheel and your eyes straight ahead.'

'Come on, boss. Johnson needs all the help he can get.'

'It's true.' Johnson was sullen. 'I hate this game.'

'Fine. You pick the game, Private.'

'Man, I haven't got time for games,' Johnson complained. 'I'm hot, I'm tired, and I'm hungry. How about we play a nice game of everybody-gets-six-months'-R-and-R?'

'Pshh.' Rodriguez laughed. 'What the hell are you gonna do with six months' R and R, fool? You got no home to go to.'

'He's lying, Major.' Johnson threw an empty water bottle at Rodriguez and hit the driver on the back of his helmet. 'He just doesn't like that when we get back to New York, I'm gonna be out clubbing every night while he's at home changing diapers. Now there's a war zone for you.'

Zaheera wondered what she would do with six months' rest and recuperation. Sit in her dingy Brooklyn apartment and wait for the break to end, probably.

'What would you do, Major?' Johnson asked.

'With what?'

'Six months, all to yourself. Budget notwithstanding. What would you do?'

'Dance with joy for every moment I'm not trapped in a moving oven with two of the smelliest pricks known to man.'

'Ah, you'd miss us too much.'

'Damned straight,' Rodriguez added. 'Major here wakes up every morning delighted to be stuck with us lot. Ain't that right, Major?'

'You sure you haven't been smoking some of the local supply, Corporal?'

'Shit, I wish.'

'I never heard that.'

The convoy stopped up ahead. Zaheera got on the radio and checked what was going on. Something about stray goats crossing the road.

'Fucking goats,' Rodriguez complained.

Zaheera opened her portable screen and checked the drone footage.

All clear so far.

'Goats!' Johnson exclaimed.

'What?' Zaheera said.

'Goats. As in goats with a G. That's it, right?'

Rodriguez laughed out loud. 'Man, how fucking stupid are you? She said inside. You see any fucking goats hopping about in here?' He pounded the steering wheel as he savoured Johnson's exasperated expression.

Zaheera scanned the horizon as best she could. This was taking too long for her liking. Roadside ambushes had caused at least fifty casualties in the last few months and Zaheera had no desire to be the fifty-first. The drone's footage didn't show anything to worry about. But then that would have been the same for the other roadside attacks. No matter how advanced an army came to Afghanistan, it didn't seem like any fared better than another to Zaheera. The hills were stained with the blood of the fallen from count-less failed attempts to tame this land. She radioed in again to see what the hold-up was and told the private on the other end that he would spend the rest of the month cleaning the latrines if they weren't on the move again soon.

His powers of persuasion must have improved rapidly in the time after their chat, because they were soon inching along again. Zaheera pulled out a notepad and jotted down the GPS coordinates for the location of their unplanned delay. She looked at the two soldiers in the vehicle with her and saw that they were trying to mask their unease as much as she was. Rodriguez's hands were practically fused to the steering wheel in a steel grip. Johnson was trying his best not to stick his head up front with them and peer out. Zaheera felt him leaning forward as subtly as he could on occasion. She tried to ease the tension by breaking out some day-old cookies she'd brought with her. 'Bagels,' she said.

'What was that, Major?' Johnson asked.

'You asked what I'd do with six months' R and R. I'd get down to my favourite bagel shop in Brooklyn every morning and stuff my face with bagels. Then I'd take a coffee and a book with me and walk over the Brooklyn Bridge into Manhattan and spend the day in Central Park.'

'That sounds nice, Major,' Rodriguez said.

'Don't you have any family in New York?' Johnson asked.

'No,' Zaheera answered. 'My mother lives in the UK.'

'You wouldn't want to visit her?' Johnson asked, not quite sensing Zaheera's tone.

'No.'

A small object hit Zaheera's windscreen and bounced off. Zaheera turned front and centre and looked for any sign of the object. A second later she knew.

'Grenade!' Rodriguez shouted and launched himself as best he could from the driver's seat to cover Zaheera.

The grenade exploded in front of the vehicle, doing minimal damage. Bits of shrapnel ricocheted off the wind-screens and bonnet while the cloud of smoke and dust blocked their vision. Zaheera heard shouting coming from the vehicles in front and behind in the convoy. They were under attack.

'Thanks,' she said to Rodriguez. 'I'm good. Get on the mic and find out what's going on.' She popped the hatch in the roof above her seat and aimed her assault rifle out across the horizon. An RPG whistled towards their section of the convoy and hit the front wheel of the vehicle in front, sending it airborne for a second before it crashed onto its side in the ditch beside the road. Zaheera saw one of the vehicles in the convoy fire two bursts in the direction she'd seen the RPG coming from. She couldn't see anything in the distance. Nothing but dust and sparse shrubbery and the relentless torture of the sun. *Why didn't the drone pick anything up?*

To her right a group of individuals appeared from behind a rock, throwing down the cloaking devices they had been wearing to avoid detection while they had waited for the convoy to cross their path. *Pretty expensive tech for resistance fighters.* Zaheera counted at least eight of them. They opened fire on the convoy. She heard Johnson climb into the harness of the heavy machine gun behind her and made a mental note to congratulate him later for his quick thinking. He let rip a hailstorm of fire at the insurgents, each shot a thunderous clap.

Zaheera saw two of the Taliban fall to the ground. The others scattered. Dust rose in every direction as bullets kicked up small clouds of dirt. Something leaked from the overturned vehicle in the ditch. Zaheera didn't want to stick around to have her worst fears confirmed. She slung her rifle over her back, leapt out of the armoured security vehicle and made a beeline for the overturned vehicle. It took two hard pulls at the door before it came loose. A soldier spilled into her arms as she looked inside, his face burned from the explosion that had flipped his troop transport vehicle. He was out cold. Zaheera pulled the unrecognisable soldier from his seat and propped him over her shoulder. The sonofabitch was heavy. She staggered sideways a couple of steps before regaining her composure and zigzagged her way across the ground, hoping to all hell that no Taliban were hiding on this side of the road. The lack of cover gave her hope that they had all hidden in the rock cover on the other side.

Thankfully no Taliban were lying in her path and no stray bullets made unwelcome appearances. She could hear the bullets hitting every vehicle in the convoy. The lead hit steel and glass in a cacophony that reminded Zaheera of those winter hailstorms in Brooklyn when she would sit up with Dad and play cards to take her mind off the crackle of the lightning.

She placed the soldier down as gently as she could and headed straight back for the rest of her team. Johnson was still in the turret unloading the taxpayers' finest into the opposition. The other gunners were firing in the same direction as Johnson. Bullet shells rained down on the ground in a brass symphony. Another RPG whistled across the Afghanistan countryside. Zaheera heard it too late. It hit the underside of the overturned troop transport vehicle and caused an explosion unlike anything she had ever seen. She was thrown from her feet, spinning in the air and landing face first in the unforgiving gravel.

Her ears rang in the aftermath of the explosion as she lay in the caked earth. *What the fuck just happened?* She gave herself a quick pat down. No limbs appeared to be missing. At least that was something. She sat up on her haunches, her head still dizzy from being thrown back with such force. Slowly her vision managed to centre itself to the point where she was only seeing double.

Zaheera heard screaming nearby. A black cloud billowed from the burning troop transport vehicle; the smell of flaming rubber and diesel filled her nostrils. She looked around again and realised the screaming was coming from inside the shell that remained of the burning vehicle, as if from victims inside a brazen bull. Zaheera forced herself to her feet and hotfooted it to the nearest door.

She recoiled in agony as her hand touched the broiling handle. It felt worse than grabbing a steel pan left on the barbeque. The sound of gunfire still filled the air. Zaheera guessed that the remaining insurgents had retreated to their rock cover and were now holding out as best they could. *Holding out and regretting their decision.* The window of the door she had just tried to access blew open as the heat proved too much. Zaheera looked inside but could see nothing through the flames and smoke.

The screaming had stopped.

Rodriguez, now standing outside the armoured security vehicle, was taking potshots round the side and intermittently lobbing what grenades he had at the opposition. Zaheera recalled him bragging on a recent march how he'd played quarterback all through college. Almost went pro, he'd claimed. *At least school taught him something.* She hopped the gap between the two vehicles and took a knee. 'Sitrep?'

'Not sure, Major Bhukari. Johnson's giving them hell but we can't hear shit on comms with all the gunfire. Looks like the two lead vehicles got hit pretty bad, too.' He pointed further up the convoy.

Only then did Zaheera realise just how bad it was. In all the chaos, she had assumed it had only been the troop transport vehicle in front of her that had been hit. Now the carnage was revealing itself. 'How many?'

'Dead? I don't know,' Rodriguez said.

'No, how many of them?'

'Hard to tell.'

He was out of breath and struggling to get the words out. Zaheera gave him a moment to gather himself and handed him her water bottle.

'I count at least fifty,' he said. 'They're spread out among the rocks. It's damn near impossible to hit them from this distance. Johnson's giving it the old college try, though.'

Shell casings rained down from above as Johnson's now hoarse voice continued to bark obscenities as he swivelled with the heavy machine gun, methodically firing in short bursts across different areas of the rock formation, barely giving the Taliban much of a chance to peek their heads out, let alone fire back.

By Zaheera's count there were still three other vehicles that hadn't been taken out, two ahead and one behind, in the convoy. She wasn't sure if everybody in them was still alive but the gunfire emitted by them meant at least *some* were. There was hope yet. 'Stay here and keep Johnson covered. I'm going to go check on the others.'

'Affirmative, Major.' Rodriguez turned and engaged the enemy once more.

Zaheera, leaving her assault rifle slung over her back, pulled out her pistol and checked it was loaded. Staying low, she lugged her aching body to the vehicle behind. 'Sergeant Miller, you all right?'

The sergeant's poker face wasn't worth shit by Zaheera's reckoning. Fear was carved into every pore on his face. He looked in over his head. She peered over his shoulder at his vehicle. Splatters of red on all the windows confirmed that she needn't ask the question. 'There's a man out there.' She pointed in the direction of the burned soldier she had carried to safety. 'I want you to haul ass over to him and keep him alive. You'll be far enough from the gunfire that you can call in air support without being drowned out.'

His eyes glazed over. Zaheera figured he was reliving whatever atrocity had just happened in that abattoir of a vehicle. She slapped him hard across the face. It did the trick. 'You listening, Sergeant?'

'Sorry, Major. Yes. Radio in for air support. Confirmed.'

He bolted across the dirt before she had a chance to give him an alternate order.

Zaheera turned around and ran the length of the convoy to the two remaining vehicles ahead of Rodriguez and Johnson. Bullets continued to rattle against the other side of the vehicles as she ran past them. A stray shot clipped the top of her helmet and sent her sprawling to the ground. Thankfully, it hadn't penetrated the helmet or anything else. For the second time that day, Zaheera bit the dirt. One of the soldiers from the vehicles she had been trying to get to leant over her and pulled her up onto her feet.

'You all right, Major Bhukari?'

'Fine, thank you, Private Ramirez.'

His face was covered in dust and blood. From what Zaheera could make out, none of the blood was his. His hands, too, were stained a dark red, almost black.

'Who?' she asked, indicating the blood on his hands and uniform.

'I forget.'

'Who's still fighting?'

'Just me.'

'Just you?'

'Just me, Major.'

'But what about the vehicle in front?'

'Just me, Major.'

The realisation they might not make it out started to sink in. She needed an exit strategy. By now, Sergeant Miller should have called in air support. The question was whether they could hold out until support came or whether it might be best to retreat to safer ground. Either way, having the remaining survivors spread out was pointless. 'Follow me,' she said, and made her way over to Sergeant Miller, who was by now sitting with the injured soldier she'd carried out of the burning vehicle.

'How is he?' she asked.

Sergeant Miller sat on his haunches and looked at the burned body beside him. 'He didn't make it.'

It was all Zaheera could do not to slap the bastard again. She pulled him up by the collar so that her face and his were only inches apart. His breath smelled like something had curled up in his mouth and died days ago. She wrinkled her nose up whilst she held her breath and stared into his apathetic eyes. There was no use trying to convince him. He didn't want to fight. Hell, he didn't have any fight in him. 'Did you at least call in air support?'

'Affirmative. Fifteen more minutes.'

Fifteen minutes was going to be a long time to hold out in the open. In lieu of a better option, though, they were just going to have to make it work. She shoved Miller in the direction of the convoy where Johnson and Rodriguez were still holding their own. He stumbled and caught himself before he went over. Zaheera knew she was being a little rough considering the scene in his vehicle when she'd found him, but now wasn't the time to give an able gunner a free ride. She marched Miller and Ramirez ahead of her and instructed them to each take one side of the armoured security vehicle when they got there. A quick check of her watch showed that they only had another hour or so of daylight left. She did not feel like spending the night out here. *Fifteen minutes, just fifteen lousy minutes and we're home free.*

Zaheera heard the bullet sink into flesh before her eyes

registered what had happened. It fizzed through the air and sank home with a wet thunk. She saw the heavy machine gun spin as the bullet threw Johnson off balance and spun him in a balletic horror. The air filled with a red mist as two more rounds buried themselves into Johnson. The kid didn't scream. But he didn't remain standing either. His body flopped in on itself and he disappeared from view as he dropped into his metal coffin below.

ZAHEERA COULDN'T REMEMBER how old Johnson had been. She knew it was eighteen or nineteen. The kid had been braver than anybody else in the convoy. While they had all scrambled to find a safe way to fight back, the kid had hopped straight into the harness of the heavy machine gun and hadn't stopped firing until that one fatal bullet found its target. *Why are the brave always the first to go?* She cursed herself for still being alive in that moment.

Zaheera dropped to the ground and fired under the vehicle at their attackers, taking care to keep most of her body hidden behind the tyre. She couldn't make out how many were still left from this distance. They were sitting ducks in the road. What would her mother say? *She'd finally be able to say she told me this would happen.*

She climbed into the driver's seat of the vehicle and got the drone's control out, doing her best not to look at Johnson's slumped body in the back. It was hot and humid inside and the air stank of warm flesh. Zaheera got herself out of the vehicle as quick as she could and slammed the door behind her. The screen showed the drone's field of vision, circling above. It counted five moving heat signatures camped out in the rocks on the other side of the road and a few other not so hot heat signatures that didn't appear to be moving. Assuming there weren't any others still hanging out under cloaking devices, Zaheera figured they still had a chance.

A distant sound of thunder rolled overhead, which sounded out of place in the baking desert heat. Air support was nearby. She ordered everybody to take cover and hoped like shit that Miller had given the right coordinates. Two jets whistled through the sky above them on their strafing run. A second later the ground where the Taliban were camped lit up like a firework display. Dust filled the air as Zaheera scanned for any survivors. Overhead, the jets circled round and lined up for another strafing run. Again she ordered everybody to remain in cover and again the ground lit up like the Fourth of July as the jets whistled past before returning to base.

Miller leapt to his feet as the jets headed home. 'Yeah. Get some,' he shouted towards the rock formation.

'Miller, get down,' she ordered.

'Take that, you lousy sonsof—'

The bullet hit him directly in the forehead. He didn't flinch or falter. Just stood there all dumbstruck for a split second with his eyes closed before he went to the ground like a sack of potatoes.

Ramirez ran out from cover to tend to Miller.

'Ramirez, no!'

Too late.

He was hit in the back as he tried to pick Miller's corpse up. Another bullet hit him as he lay there in the dirt. Whatever sadistic fuck was out there with the sniper rifle really did not want to leave any stragglers behind. Zaheera, crouched behind the front wheel of the armoured security vehicle, looked at Rodriguez crouched behind the back wheel. 'You okay?'

'Yes, Major.'

'All right, it looks like we've got a sniper on our asses. Still, it's you and me, Rodriguez, and only one of him.'

'What's the plan?'

'We need to get away from these fucking vehicles.'

'But there's no cover, Major.'

'There will be soon,' she said, tapping her watch.

Rodriguez looked towards the sun's low arch on the horizon and smiled. 'We've got this, Major.'

'Damned straight. Get your night vision goggles out of the vehicle. As soon as the sun drops over the horizon, we're going to go teach this bastard a lesson.'

RODRIGUEZ AND ZAHEERA both ate what little they had on them as the darkness set in. Zaheera chewed on an old nut bar she had been saving for the journey back but, given the circumstances, now seemed as good a time as any to chow down. She rested against the front tyre she had been sitting up against for the last few hours while Rodriguez took his turn on watch. Night vision goggles on, he lay prone in the dirt just to the left side of the rear tyre. The drone had long since been shot out of the sky by the sniper. The comms radio was still strapped to Miller's corpse only a few feet from where they lay, but unfortunately a few feet too far. It wasn't worth the risk of trying to retrieve it; Ramirez had paid the mortal price for trying to get near Miller's body. Zaheera knew that the footage from the jets would by now have been analysed back at the base and that some kind of rescue strategy would no doubt be planned or already in motion. She hoped for the latter. Until then it was going to be her and Rodriguez up against this sniper and Zaheera had no plans of letting the sniper take anybody else when they came to rescue her and Rodriguez. There was also the niggling feeling that the sniper might well have his or her own comms device and might well already have his own backup on the way. The only way to solve the problem was to end it.

She knew she should be feeling upset or scared, or a combination of both, but in truth, she felt alive. Perhaps it had something to do with the adrenaline of the afternoon's fighting, or the knowledge that there was still someone out there waiting for her to make one wrong move. Whatever it was, her nerves were on edge, her senses dialled up to the maximum, and if she was being totally honest with herself, she felt at her most comfortable. *This is where I'm supposed to be.*

Rodriguez sat silently, switching between checking his scope and checking the night vision goggles. Zaheera noticed his gooseflesh-like arms and wished they could make a fire. The desert heat had disappeared in a heartbeat and had been replaced with a bitter cold. It felt worse than Brooklyn in the winter. A fire was out of the question, though. That would unfortunately mean certain death. She tapped the ground gently to get his attention.

'What is it?' he whispered.

'Time to make our move. You stay here. I'm going to flank right. You see anything move out there that isn't coming from the right, you shoot it.'

'This is ridiculous,' he snapped back under his breath. Clearly all nerves were shot to shit and any adherence to the chain of command were now gone. This was just two people trying to survive.

Zaheera didn't like her plan any more than Rodriguez did but she wasn't about to let them die from hypothermia or let an ambush get them in the night. It was now or never.

'You want him taking potshots at anybody else when they roll up to get us, huh?' she hissed under breath. 'Just keep your eyes peeled. Shoot fast and shoot true.'

'What if I shoot you?'

'I'm hoping you'll be able to tell the difference.'

'Between a man and a woman in the dark at a hundred or more yards? You've got to be kidding.'

'You don't know it's a man. But you know I'm in fatigues. You see anybody in your sights that ain't wearing a helmet or some kind of US combat uniform, you take 'em down, you hear?'

'Yes, Major.'

'Good. Now if you don't hear anything for a while, don't come after me. You're my best chance of survival if you just stay here.'

'Affirmative.'

'Good.' She got into a prone position and started to crawl sideways on her front.

'Major?' Rodriguez asked as she crawled passed him.

'Yes?'

'Nothing. Good luck.'

'See you in a minute.'

'I'll have the fire ready.'

'See,' she smiled, though doubted whether it showed in his night vision goggles, 'I knew you'd eventually prove useful.' She inched along, careful not to make a sound, until she got to the vehicle behind hers. Hours earlier, Miller had been only too keen to depart from this spot and hunker down safely a few hundred yards back. Blood pooled on the ground where it had leaked through door seals. Zaheera gained a new respect for her attackers then. They had hit the front and rear convoy vehicles, caging in the rest and leaving them ripe for execution. That too had been done well, she had to accept, considering the vast differences in resources, although their budget had improved dramatically since her last tour in 2028. A couple of years ago, they didn't have cloaking devices. That one she had not expected. War, it seemed to Zaheera, was simply an endless battle to be the guy with the bigger stick. Whatever new technology they brought, the enemy figured out a way to counter and vice versa. At least at the end it came down to a battle of wits. Right now it was just her, the sniper, and hopefully her backup. *Forget all the technology. Forget the large armies. Forget the location, the politics, everything.* It was just hunter versus hunted. This was much more Zaheera's style. *Just like hunting deer with Dad.*

Zaheera paused as she rounded the back of the tail vehicle and gave Rodriguez a thumbs up. *No turning back now.* She removed her pistol from its holster and checked it still had a few rounds in it. Hobbling over rough terrain with a rifle in hand was going to be too noisy and she doubted she could swing the rifle into position quick enough if it came down to it. At least with a pistol she could keep it in her hand, ready to fire, and still manoeuvre without any unnecessary difficulty. The problem with a pistol and firing at a target in the dark was the guarantee of inaccuracy. In the end she decided to sling her assault rifle over her back and bring it, just in case. Her night vision goggles provided a spotty green-and-black view of the night. Nothing moved in her line of sight and so, moving even slower – if it was possible – she crept forwards into the ditch on the other side of the road. There were no more vehicles to protect her. Barely any shrubbery, either. Thankfully the ground was fairly uneven and interspersed with small and medium-sized rocks. In between the rocks on occasion were small shrubs – completely ineffective to stop firepower if it came down to it, but potentially at least cover as she crawled along the ground towards the sniper. Zaheera hoped it would be enough. She thought of how she would tell others about this if she made it out alive. Most of the people she'd have any interest in talking to were lying behind her in their own blood. Nobody back in New York would understand the day's events in any real way and there was no way she going all the way to the UK after this to see her mother, only to be told again how ridiculous this career choice was. At least there was Rodriguez. Zaheera hoped he still had her back.

The ground was still warm beneath her. Nearby a hare shuffled slowly through the night looking for shrubbery to eat. It paused every moment or so and raised its head to check for predators. *That's what happens when you don't have backup.* Zaheera crawled forward again, careful not to spook the hare.

She made it to the rock formation without any further sightings. The air smelled of blood and faeces. Flies buzzed around, taking advantage of the feast on offer. Zaheera held her breath as she moved through the rocks, breathing through her mouth when she absolutely had to in order to try and stifle the pungent aroma of rotting flesh that filled her nose. There was no escaping it, though. She wondered how the sniper had stayed here all day, lying among his or her fallen comrades, whether he or she was as on edge as she was. She hoped so.

Something moved up ahead and Zaheera aimed the pistol in its direction. She readied herself to fire.

Silence.

She crawled forward again, keeping the direction of the sound she'd heard in mind. The cold Afghan night was lit by a half moon. Not quite enough to work without the night vision goggles but enough, she thought, that the sniper might still be able to get the jump on her if she was spotted first. A big boulder ahead offered her the chance to get up into a crouched position. She waited a moment until her breathing steadied. This wasn't a moment for shaky hands.

Something scraped against tin. The sniper was eating. The sound came from the other side of the boulder. Zaheera placed her pistol back into its holster and pulled her assault rifle from her back. *Less requirement for accuracy.* She kept close to the boulder, rifle out in front and ready to end the sonofabitch.

The tin scraped again. This was her chance. She leapt out from the cover of the boulder and pulled the trigger.

Nothing happened.

Fucking piece of shit.

The rifle had jammed. Whether it was dust or just a mechanical failure, she would never know.

The guy sat in front of her rolled to his side, grabbed his own weapon and fired two shots. Both hit Zaheera in the stomach. She staggered back, right hand reaching for her pistol.

The guy pulled the trigger again but this time Zaheera only heard a soft click.

Empty.

She fell to the ground, her night vision goggles disconnecting from her helmet and crashing off into the dirt somewhere behind her.

The sniper pulled a knife from his belt and leapt on top of her, bringing the blade down with his full weight behind him. Zaheera covered her face with both arms in an X and let out a scream as the blade sliced through her forearm, sending the pistol from her grip in the process. A white hot flash of pain shot through her. She did the only thing she could think of and brought her knee up into his balls.

He keeled over with a teen-like squeal and grabbed at his bruised manhood in agony.

Zaheera heard what she hoped was Rodriguez running over the ground and up the rocks to her. He called out in the night.

She rolled over and saw the pistol between her and the sniper. He noticed it too. Her vision was becoming blurred with the loss of blood. The two bullets in her stomach and knife in her arm hadn't exactly levelled the playing field. In the end, the sniper had been much quicker than her.

Rodriguez came bounding over the rocks without a care for his own safety. He'd clearly heard her scream and wasn't about to let any more time go by. He met the sniper face on and emptied the entire clip into the sniper's chest.

Not before the sniper got a shot off, though.

Zaheera saw Rodriguez's neck darken as he dropped onto his back.

Everything went silent.

Somewhere in the distance she heard a wolf howl.

She lay on her back and admired the stars.

So this is how it ends. At least Mom can say she told me so.

2

The minibus pulled into the gates of the rehabilitation centre in Surrey, just south of London. It had been six weeks since Zaheera had sustained near-fatal injuries in Afghanistan and had been flown to a city called Birmingham in the United Kingdom where she had been treated. She had never been to Birmingham before in her life but she'd looked it up on a map the first chance she got. It turned out to be only a few hours from London, where her mother resided. As a result, she had refused family visits. There wasn't a chance in hell she was going to let her mother see her in that state, all bruised and bloodied, with drips and tubes running all over her body. Whatever parts of her body hadn't been embedded with tubes and machinery had been bandaged. It had been a couple of weeks before she'd even been able to get out of bed and over to the bathroom to get a good look at herself in the mirror.

It hadn't been a pretty sight. Her long dark hair had been dirty and unwashed, her face bruised and puffy. Her arm had hurt like hell, more so than her stomach, she'd thought. The doctors had told her that the army medics in Afghanistan had managed to remove the two bullets in her stomach but that they hadn't had the benefits of the medical facilities she now found herself in, and therefore they had been forced to do a further operation to stitch up some internal wounds and clear out some infected tissue.

Zaheera hadn't asked about her team at all during the six weeks in Birmingham. She didn't need to. The doctors hadn't been too happy about her request to deny any visitors and told her that it was best she re-engage with society as soon as possible. They had said that any loved ones who could lighten the burden for her would help her recovery. What did they know, though? She thought of Johnson up on the heavy machine gun, Rodriguez leaping over the rocks to come save her, Ramirez lying in the dirt as he'd tried to get to Miller. There was nothing to do to lighten their burdens now.

The rehabilitation centre reminded Zaheera of a grand English manor, like the ones so often pictured in film and television. It was a large red-brick mansion covered in ivy, with many chimneys and surrounded by vast lawns. If Birmingham had reminded Zaheera of some of the Brooklyn projects then this place was clearly the Hamptons. The long gravel driveway took the minibus past a few outbuildings. Places of residence for butlers and whatnot, no doubt. All around, the mansion was surrounded by vast green fields. Zaheera even spotted a river at the bottom of the field directly in front of the mansion. She pushed her face up to the window to get the best view. She breathed in the smell of freshly cut grass and, for the first time in six weeks, Zaheera allowed herself to indulge in her surroundings. It felt good to be out of hospital, to be up and about again.

'Fucking hell, are they playing croquet?' asked one of

Zaheera's fellow passengers.

The three of them hadn't said a word to each other since getting in the minibus together at the hospital. One of them had lost a leg, presumably on a landmine, although Zaheera couldn't bring herself to ask, while the other's face was severely burned. He reminded her of the soldier she'd pulled from the troop transport vehicle after it had been hit by the RPG. She had spent the entire journey trying not to look at him. By comparison her own injuries didn't seem too bad. Although the weeks spent wallowing in her bed hadn't prepared her for the possibility that others might have left Afghanistan in a worse state than herself.

Zaheera looked at the soldiers in the field that the burned soldier had pointed out. They were playing croquet. Some of them had obvious injuries, some of them less so. They looked to her like they were having a good time, though. She wondered how long they had all been here. The minibus pulled up outside the front of the mansion where its passengers were met by a doctor of sorts. He looked ex-military. Zaheera took in his hard frame hiding behind the white lab coat and slacks.

'Welcome,' he said to the three of them as they stepped out of the minibus, 'to Harley Manor.' He signalled for some other soldiers to come out from the big wooden doors behind him. 'I'm Doctor Griffiths.'

Zaheera and her two fellow passengers nodded awkwardly, unsure of quite what to do with themselves.

'I know you've each been through incredible trauma recently. Everybody here at Harley Manor, including many like yourselves, is here to help.'

They muttered their thanks and were ushered along with the doctor's helpers to their room. The three of them were put in a large bedroom with four single beds. Each bed was in a corner of the room, with a wooden locker beside it. It would have passed for a military barracks if everything didn't look so comfortable and plush. The single beds had thick, inviting mattresses, with white bedsheets and two pillows. *Two pillows!* Each pine locker looked big enough to hold enough kit for a year, let alone a few weeks. The high ceilings and large windows invited plenty of light into the room and, as Zaheera peered out of the window, she noticed a small river at the bottom of the field in front of the mansion, or manor as they put it here.

One of the beds by the window was occupied by a young guy who introduced himself as Jerry. He was a young British Royal Marine. According to him this place used only to be used for British troops, but with the war in Afghanistan creating an endless stream of casualties, the Americans had partnered up with the Brits and were now sending many of their wounded here for rehabilitation before sending them home to the US. Zaheera took the other bed by the window opposite Jerry's whilst the other two took the two beds against the other wall. They each unpacked quietly and then sat on the ends of their beds, unsure of what to say.

'What are your names?' Jerry asked when he apparently could take the solemn silence no longer.

'Major Zaheera Bhukari,' Zaheera said.

'Oh, we don't really bother with rank and all that tosh here,' Jerry replied. 'The doctors here want us to get to know each other on a first-name basis. More humane, apparently.'

'Dave,' the one-legged soldier said, shaking Jerry's hand.

'Pleasure to meet you, Dave.'

Dave's accent was British, although somewhat different to Jerry's. She'd never quite heard anything like it before. It was nothing like the British accents she was accustomed to on TV. Dave was quite a big guy, with round shoulders and a bald head so shiny it would only require three small holes placed in a triangle to make a serviceable bowling ball. He looked uncomfortable leaning on his crutches, with his half-leg bandaged up at the stump.

'Kendrick,' the burned one said. His dark skin was patched with pink where the burns had disfigured him. What remained of his original skin had a reflective sheen to it.

Zaheera caught herself staring again and looked away. There wasn't any protocol for addressing the wounded. Training had only ever been provided for treating a wound in the field but nobody had ever said what the correct course of action was when presented with somebody wounded off the battlefield. The others appeared to be thinking something similar as they shuffled their feet like kids in a dormitory on the first day of school.

'Well, let me show you around, then,' Jerry said, clearly desperate to ease the awkwardness.

They followed him around the manor as he delivered his tour, divulging history on certain rooms and the paint-ings or military paraphernalia hanging within. One room contained a sword from the Battle of Waterloo, although its previous owner was unknown. In one room, which Jerry introduced as the library, despite the fact that the total volume of books stood at fewer than twenty, a bolt-action rifle from the Battle of the Somme was displayed on the wall above the fireplace. Everywhere, it seemed, there was some testament to death. Zaheera found it hard, as Jerry droned on with such pride in the various military conflicts, not to consider the families of those killed, let alone survivors who'd had to witness the atrocities and then carry them with them the rest of their lives. Six weeks on from the attack on her convoy and Zaheera was not dealing any better with the loss of her fellow soldiers. Each moment was dulled almost to a silence, as if the real world were only a whisper above the explosions and gunfire still going off in her head. She could still hear the RPG hitting the troop transport vehicle in front of her, the sand falling like a light rain on the scorched earth. Her skin crawled with unreleased anger: anger at not being taken out with her team; anger at having to live on in shame, as if she had somehow not quite given enough; anger at an enemy she didn't choose; anger at those who had sent her and her team to fight a war that could never be won.

'Zaheera?'

'Hmm?' She looked round and noticed Jerry smiling that knowing smile she had already come to despise from her doctors. It looked even worse on a soldier. That *I've-been-there-too* smile, yet he hadn't. Whatever Jerry's battle had been, it hadn't been out on that road with her team. What did Jerry fucking know?

'You all right?' he asked.

The others had stopped in their tracks too.

'Yeah, fine. Sorry. Just admiring the view,' she lied.

Jerry nodded. 'Shall we get some scran?'

He led the way to the dining hall.

The gunfire and explosions in Zaheera's head followed her all the way to the hall and all the way back to their room afterwards. She took a couple sleeping pills before putting her head down that night to make sure she knocked herself out.

ZAHEERA WOKE with a start in the night. Her bedsheets clung to her sweat-drenched body. She looked around in the dark to see what had woken her. The full moon shone through the window, providing a little light. Outside, an owl hooted gently from a nearby tree. Zaheera got out of bed and pulled the dressing gown she had been given earlier over her pyjamas. There was no point trying to go back to sleep. The pills might have helped with knocking her out but her nightmares had not dissipated. She slipped into her running shoes and looked about the room. Dave lay on his back against one wall snoring so loudly Zaheera wondered whether that was what had caused his bad luck in Afghanistan. Any enemy within a hundred miles would be alerted to a racket like that. His duvet lay in a heap on the floor and Zaheera was spared any unseemly view thanks to a sheet that managed to just about cover some of Dave's stomach and lower body. Kendrick, on the other hand, lay quietly in his bed, with just his head out from the duvet. Jerry's bed was empty.

She crept out of the room and headed for the library, stopping on the way for the toilet, wherein she heard someone crying in a cubicle. Apparently Zaheera wasn't the only one struggling with sleep in this place. She splashed her face with cold water and left the grieving individual to battle his own monsters alone.

Jerry was sitting by the window in the library, gazing out at the night when she entered. 'Beautiful here, isn't it?'

'Yes,' she said. 'I'm sorry, I didn't mean to disturb you.'

'No, no, that's quite all right. Gives me something other than my own thoughts to deal with.'

At his invitation, Zaheera made her way into the room and examined some of the books on the shelf. She had expected some self-help books, or true stories from soldiers who'd made it through severe injury to a normal life afterwards, but she found only regular fiction. Lewis Carroll, Shakespeare, Dickens, Kipling, Tolstoy, Shelley. Despite feeling that it was still too few books to dub the room a library, she was now pleased with the collection of books it housed. At the very least, she could revisit some of the books she'd read in her teens. Perhaps that was their purpose – to take one back to a simpler time. She noticed that Jerry had been attempting to read Melville but had spurned the adventures of Ahab and Ishmael in favour of stargazing. The book lay open on his lap, spine up to save his page.

'Can't sleep?' he asked Zaheera.

'Sleeping pills didn't do the trick.'

'Ah, don't worry about that. They give you much stronger stuff here, if that's what you're after.'

'I'd rather just have a good night's sleep.'

'Wouldn't we all.' He stood up from his seat and pushed the window up, placing his book on the windowsill. 'Cigarette?' he asked, pulling out a packet of rolling tobacco from his pocket.

'Sure,' she replied, berating herself for picking up a habit she thought she had managed to kick. No matter what she tried, she never seemed further than one bad day from picking it up again. Today happened to be just such a day.

Jerry rolled two cigarettes and handed one to Zaheera. She cupped her hands around the tip as he lit it for her and she took a couple of short pulls to make sure it was lit. Then she took one long pull on it. *There it is.* It amazed her that the effect was always so instant, like the body was just waiting for the next hit. An instant feeling of calm took over her as the reintroduction to her old friend made her a little light-headed. She sat on the windowsill opposite Jerry and blew the smoke out into the night. 'We allowed to smoke in here?'

'I won't tell if you won't.'

'Deal.'

They both sat quietly for a minute, savouring their cigarettes and each other's company. Zaheera heard a fox bark somewhere nearby, it's high-pitched yip breaking her new-found serenity.

'What's keeping you up?' Jerry asked, stubbing the cigarette out on the windowsill and placing the butt back in his rolling tin.

'A variety of things, I guess,' she said, trying to evade any further conversation on the topic.

'Right,' he nodded. 'Well, when you're ready to talk, I'm here.'

'Thanks,' she said. 'How long have you been here?'

'Six months.'

'Christ, when the hell do we get out of here?'

'Oh, you'll probably be gone in a few weeks. Don't worry about it. Once you're physically fit for battle, you'll be shipped straight back. Failing that, you'll be shipped home.'

'Forgive me for asking, but in that case, why are you still here?'

'I'm what they call a hazard to myself.' He pulled up one sleeve and showed Zaheera the scars on the inside of his right arm and smiled sheepishly before pulling the sleeve back down again and patting it to make sure it stayed in place.

'I'm so sorry.'

'Don't worry about it,' he said. 'I realised after a few attempts that I couldn't even get that right.' He starting rolling himself another cigarette. 'Figured that here's as good as any other place to hang out for a while.'

'Where do you live normally?' she asked.

'Well, I was based in Germany before Afghanistan, but my family home is in Oxford, if that's what you mean. I suppose I'll head back there once I'm discharged from this place. It's all right here, though, once you get used to the others crying at night or getting a bit physical on occasion.'

'Physical?'

'Every once in a while someone thinks they're still in battle and ends up attacking whichever unlucky soul they think is the enemy.' He looked at Zaheera. 'If I'm being honest, you might want to keep an eye out.'

'My skin colour and my surname have been getting me into unwanted trouble long before I got here, but thanks, I appreciate the heads-up.' She accepted a second cigarette from Jerry. 'So what do we actually do here?'

'Meetings and physio, mostly. Depends on the injury, you know?'

She did.

'Me, I spend a lot of time in meetings. My guess is you'll do the same. Dave and Kendrick both probably have a fair bit of physio to get through, Dave especially.'

Zaheera wasn't particularly excited about the prospect of meetings. She imagined some kind of AA-type meeting, where everybody sat around in a circle and acknowledged each other's inadequacies. She wasn't in the mood for baring all to a group of strangers, no matter what military background they might all have in common. None of them were from her battalion and therefore none of them had shared her particular experience of the war. There would be no point even trying to explain what she had been through.

'Well, that's me,' Jerry said. 'Just needed a few cigarettes to calm the nerves. Thanks for the chat.'

'Yeah, you too. And thanks for the cigarettes.'

'No worries.'

Zaheera waited until Jerry had left the room before she turned back towards the night. She wasn't ready to go back to bed just yet. The nightmares could wait.

3

'Do you want to tell me about it?' Dr Griffiths asked.

'Tell you about what?' Zaheera asked.

They were sitting in his office, Dr Griffiths behind his large oak desk in a rather decadent swivel chair, Zaheera on a leather single couch opposite him. She'd opted against the awful bed-thing she'd expected and was somewhat repulsed to see actually being used by shrinks. The room was covered in bookshelves stocked with leather-bound volumes of important-looking medical titles.

'They should call this the library,' she said.

'What was that?'

'Nothing.'

He wrote something down.

Zaheera furrowed her brow. 'You going to get the pictures with the squiggly lines out and ask me what I see? I can give you a hint: it's squiggly fuckin' lines.'

He didn't respond to her jest. Instead, he asked how her room was and whether she needed anything else that could help with her comfort.

'I just want to know when I can get out of here,' she said.

'I can promise you I have no intention of keeping you here a day longer than is absolutely necessary,' he said. 'You're still recovering from the bullet wounds in your stomach and the knife wound in your arm. Physically, I'd expect you to be okay in a few weeks. But I don't want to clear you for active duty before you're ready.'

Zaheera couldn't argue with that. She didn't want to return to active duty, not that she'd admit that to this prick. The idea of heading back to Afghanistan and facing the reality of most of her regiment being either KIA or severely injured was not something she was in any rush to do. She knew from the few reports she'd been given whilst in Birmingham that her regiment had suffered multiple losses in more attacks since the attack on her convoy and, subsequently, there was talk of her regiment being brought back from tour earlier than previously planned.

'Have you had a chance to get to know your room-mates at all yet?' he asked.

'Oh, they're great,' she said. 'The bald one snores like some beast from a folk tale, the other one keeps looking at me funny, even though his face looks like someone put the character creation settings to random in a video game, and the other guy looks like he's been living in that room so long he should be paying rent.'

'They're good people,' Dr Griffiths said. 'Going through the same thing as you.'

'Sure.' Zaheera scratched at an invisible spot on her trousers. 'Why here?' she asked.

'What do you mean?'

'Why the UK? Why wasn't I sent home, or to Germany? I thought Germany was the usual destination for people in my situation.'

'Germany's a bit full at the minute,' Dr Griffiths

answered. 'As for the US, that's only if we think you're at risk of not making it. I'm happy to say that most US soldiers sent to Birmingham for treatment tend to live. Those that have been coming here over the last few years after their initial treatment have appreciated the neutral ground. It serves as a place to get yourself ready for your next step. Whether that's going home or heading back to the front line, you can at least use Harley Manor as a base without ties to your old life. Your immediate family can be flown here to be with you for short periods if you wish.' When Zaheera showed no desire to take the bait, he asked her whether there was anyone she'd like flown out to see her.

She declined.

'No family at all?' he asked.

'My mother is already based in the UK.'

Dr Griffiths admitted that he had glanced at her military records and was aware of her mother as her next of kin. 'I believe you declined any visitors whilst you were in Birmingham?'

'Would you want anybody to see you in that state?' she asked.

'I think in that state, I'd be happy just to see someone I love.'

Zaheera got up from her chair and walked over to the wall. There were a number of framed medical qualifications and certificates of sorts. 'Afraid someone's going to think you're not legit?'

'Oh, I downloaded all those from the web. Makes me feel like I know what I'm talking about.'

Zaheera remained facing the wall. She didn't want to reward his witticism with a reaction.

'Can I get you a coffee?'

'Hmm?'

'You know, black drink. Some people put milk and sugar in it, although I'm not sure those kinds of people can be trusted.'

Zaheera failed to catch her smile before it broke out across her face. Dr Griffiths saw this and softened in his chair. Maybe he wasn't so bad. 'Thanks, that'd be great,' she said, accepting the truce.

He poured her a mug from his cafetière and offered her milk and sugar, which she promptly declined, following his prior character evaluation. 'Do you want to tell me about it?' he said, leaning back in his chair and taking a sip from his own mug.

'I wouldn't know where to start.'

'That's fair. Look, you don't have to say anything today if you don't want to, but the sooner we can have an honest conversation with each other, the sooner we can get you to where you need to be. Personally, I don't mind whether that's back home to the States or back to Afghanistan. I just want to help.'

'Why?'

'Because I saw what this shit did to my father and subsequently my mother and I swore to myself that if I could help even one person, that'd at least be something.'

'Have you?'

'I hope so.'

Zaheera sipped her coffee. She wasn't even trying to give him a hard time anymore. She actually didn't know where to start with this shit. Right now, getting a good night's sleep was a concern. But she didn't really want to talk about how she woke up thinking she was still among the rocks with Rodriguez running to save her, only to be shot down in front of her, his eyes still open in the night, while she lay there on the ground, waiting to die.

'I've been told your injuries were sustained on a patrol. How did that day start?' he asked.

'We were on a routine patrol, about twenty miles from the FOB and headed back in that direction. We'd met up with another of our teams and were all headed back in convoy for the last stretch. I was in an armoured security vehicle with a driver and a gunner. The gunner, Johnson, was waxing lyrical about what he'd do with a bit of R and R. He was just a kid.'

'And what happened?'

'We were passing a rocky outcrop when it all kicked off. The drone above us never picked anything up. The Taliban had upgraded a lot of their equipment since my last tour a couple of years ago. Some figures popped out from nowhere, throwing down these cloaking devices they had been using. It looked more modern than what we had. They must have secured some extra funding recently.'

'So you were ambushed?'

'Yeah. First I knew of it was a grenade bouncing off the front of my vehicle and exploding in the dirt. The driver, Rodriguez, leapt over from his seat and covered me as best he could.' Zaheera paused, smiling at the memory. 'Crazy fool cared about anybody but himself. Anyway, that's when it all went to shit. And pretty quickly, too. Next thing I know, an RPG blew up the troop transport vehicle just in front of us. Sent the vehicle crashing into the ditch. I jumped out to see if anybody had survived the explosion while the others engaged the enemy. We fought for what felt like hours but in reality, I'm guessing, it was probably a few minutes. They had the front and rear vehicles pinned in. There was nothing we could do except call in for air support and try to survive as best we could.'

She left out the bit about Miller being completely hopeless. No need for this guy to know. 'Air support eventually arrived but we'd taken a lot of hits just lying in the road. The air support did two strafing runs so I thought we were good, but some bastard sniper survived. Just lay there in the rocks picking us off. He took out Johnson on the gun. The kid had fought from the very first moment it had kicked off. If he hadn't been so quick and fearless, we wouldn't have lasted as long as we did. Not that it mattered in the end.'

The doctor wrote a few short notes as Zaheera continued to talk, but didn't interrupt.

'Anyway,' she said, 'there was no way we were going to last with him taking potshots at us. By then, almost everybody had been gunned down. It was just Rodriguez and me. I told him to stay where he was and I went after the sniper.'

'You headed straight for the rocky outcrop?'

'Not in broad daylight. We waited until the sun went down, which wasn't long – it was late afternoon when we'd first been attacked.'

'How did it feel?'

'What, waiting for dark?'

'Lying there among your fallen comrades?'

Zaheera dismissed the comment with a smirk. 'When the enemy is out there, watching, waiting for you to make the slightest mistake, you don't really have time to process or mourn the loss of your comrades. You lie there, thinking about backup, about how many rounds are left in your weapon. You think about how you're going to get out of there. You wanna know what I did while I waited for the cover of darkness? I ate a nut bar. Tasted damned good, too, if a little stale.'

'You weren't angry about Johnson?'

'Sure I was angry about Johnson. I'd gladly have traded

places with him. He didn't deserve to go out like that on a dusty road in the middle of nowhere.'

'You don't think he knew what he'd signed up for?'

'We all know what we fuckin' signed up for, you pretentious prick. Just because we signed up for it doesn't mean we gotta be put to the sword for nothing at all. You ask any soldier how they think they'll go out. Some of 'em won't discuss it at all. Some of 'em might give you some wannabe-nonchalant evasive answer. Anybody who actually spends a second or more on it will tell you they want to go out on top. They hope that if the day ever comes that their shift is ended, they want to go out grenade in one hand, rifle in the other, unloading everything they got on some unsuspecting enemy who had it coming. I guarantee you not a single soldier ever thinks that they're going to go out by stepping on a landmine, or falling from a drop rope, or any other inconvenient and unremarkable way.'

'Why is that?'

'Because we didn't sign up to be unremarkable. Most signed up to make something of themselves.'

ZAHEERA HAD LEFT her meeting with Dr Griffiths in a bit of a storm. She refused to apologise. He had probed, so he had no right to expect a civil conversation. That being said, Zaheera couldn't help but take her guilt out on her next meeting. Her physical trainer may not have expected much from her in a first session but Zaheera had pushed to her absolute limit. She needed to burn through the anger. It felt good to feel the pain again. Made her feel alive again. By the end of her afternoon session her bullet wounds were bleeding onto her shirt and her arm felt like it was on fire. The PT had called time on their exercise and said that whilst he was impressed with her dedication, he wanted her to take it easier in her next session with him. She had returned to her room grateful for having been able to blow off a little steam.

Again her sleep that night was interrupted by visions of the attack. The bloody mist that had settled over her armoured security vehicle as Johnson twirled like a ballet dancer before flopping ungracefully through the harness and into the vehicle. In her visions it happened a lot slower than it had in reality. She could almost feel the blood spatter on her face. In this nightmare the attack happened all out of order, like a highlights reel that played only the worst parts. One second Johnson was twirling with the heavy machine gun, the next Rodriguez was crashing to the earth in the rocky outcrop, his eyes refusing to close as he lay there in the dirt. Explosions went off all around her and she awoke shaking and sweat-drenched as she had the night before.

She got up and went to the toilet, taking no notice of whether any of her room-mates were still in their beds. Thankfully the toilets were not occupied with sobbing soldiers tonight. Zaheera splashed her face and behind her neck with cold water. Her reflection did not give her any comfort. She was gaunt, her cheeks hollowed out, although her eyes looked puffy and unrested, with panda-like blemishes underneath. At some point during the last few weeks she had become a ghost of herself and she couldn't figure out when. At a loss with what to do with herself, and not wanting to look at her depressing reflection any longer, she left the bathroom and went for a walk in the night.

The grounds were cool in the night air; a soft breeze blew and the trees twisted and turned ever so gently as Zaheera walked the fields around the manor. The trunks made little popping sounds as if someone nearby were cracking their knuckles. Keen not to get lost, Zaheera kept the manor in view at all times as she made her loop around the fields. Whilst she walked, she thought about Dr Griffiths' suggestion that her time here at Harley Manor would take her either home to New York or back to the battlefield in Afghanistan. She had no idea what she would do with herself if she went back to New York. Despite Johnson's question on the day of the attack, she had no real answer for what she would do with that R and R. Being a soldier was everything to Zaheera. She didn't want to do anything else. Everything about military life worked for her. They were well matched. She liked the structure, the fitness, the camaraderie, the fact that she wasn't chained to a desk. But she didn't want to do that job without the ones she knew. Learning a bunch of new faces, faces that weren't Rodriguez or Johnson. It wouldn't be the same. Somehow, it would be a betrayal to them.

Zaheera was grateful that her injuries had kept her in hospital so long that she'd likely missed all the funerals. She cursed herself for this weakness but the idea of having to acknowledge that much loss devastated her. No, there was definitely no way she could return to Afghanistan. At least, not for a while.

Hearing the trickle of the river, Zaheera was drawn towards it. The sound of the water lapping up against the riverbank soothed her and, right now, anything that helped ease her nerves was not to be dismissed. She perched on the edge of the riverbank and huddled her arms around her knees. The ground was cold and wet but it didn't matter. Anything was better than being back in her bed, terrified of the impending nightmares. She wiped a tear from her cheek, grateful that nobody was around to witness it.

A light thud nearby caught her attention. At first she

thought nothing of it as she sat gazing out in the darkness as what little light there was bounced off the ripples of water, but then it happened again. It sounded like something soft tapping wood. Wiping both eyes, just in case somebody nearby was about to run into her, she stood up and went in search of the sound. The wind rustling through the trees and river's constant flow didn't help. She had to stop every few steps until she heard it again. *It could be an unlocked door*, she thought.

Thump.

It was louder this time. She was getting closer. The hairs on the back of her neck stood up. She pushed through the overhanging branches of an old willow tree by the riverside and screamed.

She didn't need to check whose body it was; she knew the minute she saw it.

As fast as her feet could carry her, Zaheera dashed across the field back to the manor and told a nurse on duty that Jerry's body was down by the river. He had finally managed to do the one thing he said he couldn't.

This time Zaheera didn't care who saw the tears fall.

ZAHEERA SAT in a chair in reception for an hour as various people rushed in and out of the manor. Police lights and then ambulance lights filled the courtyard with a dazzling display of blue and red. A more sombre rave there couldn't exist. When her tears eventually stopped and her eyes were raw from all the rubbing, Zaheera got up and took a paper and pen from the receptionist. She looked out of the front doors and saw Jerry's body being loaded into the back of the ambulance on a stretcher as the police spoke to a shaken Dr Griffiths.

'The police should be through to speak to you when they're done with Dr Griffiths,' the receptionist said.

Zaheera grunted something indecipherable in reply.

The receptionist smiled and looked at the piece of paper Zaheera was furiously scratching over with her pen. 'What are you writing, pet?'

'My resignation.'

Zaheera woke feeling empty. Empty over the loss of Jerry. Even though she had barely got to know him, she felt like they had shared a lifetime in the library the other night. She felt empty too at the future loss of her career. She knew she'd still have to serve out her notice for the next year, but writing her resignation was the nail in the coffin for her. There had never been a plan B. No other career had been considered, despite her mother's best efforts. Her father had been delighted, of course, and Zaheera had revelled in his delight. *What would he think of me now? Cowardly? Running from the fight?* The truth was she had no fight left in her. When you know, you know. She needed to get out of the manor, serve her time, and be gone.

Strangely, to Zaheera, the previous evening's news didn't prevent the schedule from running to plan today. Although, why would it? It was just like being on tour. The whole operation just keeps trucking along. Her short stay at the manor had led her to believe it was different to the usual kind of military operation but this clearly wasn't the case.

Her first meeting that morning was with Dr Griffiths. He

looked haggard from the events of the previous evening. His shirt hadn't been ironed, his hair uncombed, although some attempt had been made to pat it down, presumably with a splash of water if the damp spots were any indication. He sat hunched over the desk in his chair while he finished typing something as Zaheera came in and took her place in the seat opposite him. The screen's reflection only highlighted his unrested and strained face.

Zaheera hoped her eyes didn't look as bad as his, although she knew that was hoping for a lot. 'Did they keep you up all night?' she asked.

He smiled, turning his attention to her. It at least rejuvenated his face somewhat. 'Not all night, no. How are you feeling about it? We barely got a chance to talk last night.'

'I'm all right,' she lied. 'It wasn't exactly what I was expecting to find on an evening stroll, though.'

'Quite. Had you had much of a chance to get to know Jerry?'

'Perhaps more than anyone else here so far, yourself excluded, of course. He seemed so cheerful.'

'They always do. Part of the reason I knew he wasn't ready to leave here.'

'Have you told his family?'

'Yes. They'll be here at some point this afternoon, I expect.'

Zaheera made a mental note to make herself scarce in the afternoon. Seeing a grieving family was not something she wanted to face just yet. They would no doubt have questions for her if it was let slip that she had been the one to find Jerry in the tree. She had dealt with many grieving families in her career, but the sheer volume of loss over the last few weeks was too much. There was no way she could face any families right now.

'I hear you were writing some kind of resignation last night,' he said.

Zaheera shifted in her seat. Her mouth tasted of acid, as if her betrayal of the only career she had ever known was now causing some kind of physical reaction. 'Yes.'

'Have you submitted it to your commander yet?'

'I wrote it up as an email before breakfast, yes.'

'Okay. I assume it will take some time to be reviewed. Out of curiosity, how long did you have left on your commission?'

'A year. I have every intention of serving out that year.'

'How do you feel?'

The acid tasted bitter in her mouth. She swallowed and put on her best poker face. 'Better.'

'Really? I always find that those I speak to after handing in their notice tend to feel some kind of guilt. It's perfectly reasonable. The military life sort of implies a lifelong commitment. Despite the turnover being quite high, I find that moments like these still tend to elicit feelings of guilt on behalf of those who want to leave.'

'Hmm.' Zaheera stared at Dr Griffiths. He offered a gentle, empathetic smile. 'Would you want to go back?'

'I couldn't,' he said. 'Used to be a medic. I saw enough to lose faith in humanity. It was too much for me. I couldn't believe we were capable of doing that to each other.'

'So you came to work here?'

'After a few more years of studying in other disciplines, yes. I wanted to help those who had been as traumatised as I had. I wanted to show them it was possible to come back from this.' He shuffled through some papers on his desk, looking somewhat uncomfortable, as if he dreaded having to deliver the next sentence. 'Zaheera, I, uhh, I hope you're not going to be too displeased, but I have asked your mother to come and visit you today.'

'You did what?'

'I know you have been refusing visitors since you've been in the UK, but I think it's time you spoke to someone who wasn't some kind of medical or military personnel.'

'My mother designs weapons for military use.'

'Yes, well, she's still your mother and, in my experience, there's nothing like having someone who can call you on your bullshit, or understand just what's eating at you, as a family member. I think it would be good for you to talk to her.'

Shit.

ZAHEERA SPENT the rest of the morning in what her mother would call a bit of a tiff. She showered and washed her hair, putting it into a plait once it had dried. One of the nurses was kind enough to lend her some moisturiser and a few other essentials. A touch of foundation and eyeliner later and Zaheera felt a little better about facing her mother. Thankfully, the foundation did a good job of putting a bit more colour into her face, which had lost its usual ochre palette as a result of being mostly indoors for weeks with only artificial light. The make-up irritated her skin but she forced herself to persevere. *Different battle armour for different occasions.*

She found her mother downstairs in reception enjoying a chat with Dr Griffiths. Her mother seemed quite taken with the doctor, at one point resting her hand on his shoulder whilst laughing at something he said. *Fucking hell, Mom. Better save the poor bastard.*

When she saw Zaheera, though, her mother's expression

instantly turned to one of concern and then relief as she rushed over and embraced her daughter tightly.

Zaheera let the embrace go on for longer than she cared to admit to herself. 'Hey, Mom,' she said, doing her best not to sob hysterically.

Her mother, showing no such restraint, wept openly as she held Zaheera. 'It's so good to see you. I told you this would happen one day. I told you not to follow your father into this wretched career but you just wouldn't listen. Now look what's happened.'

Zaheera, eyeing Dr Griffiths over her mother's shaking shoulders, cocked an eyebrow knowingly at him. 'See.'

He smiled and said nothing.

Eventually, once Zaheera had managed to get her mother back under control, she led the way up to the library. She wasn't in the mood to show her the room and have her question every aspect of what was comfortable or not, and whether she was being taken care of adequately enough. It would all be too much to handle and right now she was happier than she had expected to see her mother, so she didn't want to ruin the moment by losing her patience and snapping at her over some veiled remark regarding her tidiness or other equally insignificant point. No, the library was a neutral space from which Zaheera would be spared many potential parental barbs. Not all, of course, but it would help.

'You call this a library?' her mother asked when Zaheera led her into the room.

'It houses many of the classics.'

'It houses nothing. Where are the books?'

Zaheera gestured with one hand towards the shelf containing the books she'd perused previously. Jerry had clearly returned his copy of *Moby Dick*, which now sat alongside the other books. 'It's not the biggest collection, I'll admit. But you might recall Dad and I reading a few of these titles in the past.'

'Always with your dad. I was there too, you know. I read you some of those books too.'

'Sorry.'

Her mother waved away Zaheera's apology with a swish of her hand. All was forgiven.

Zaheera was always fascinated by her mother's ability to forgive with such ease. Perhaps that was what being a parent was. She wasn't sure. There were some things her mother held on to with a ferocity that beggared belief. Like Zaheera's joining the military. That one had never been forgotten, nor forgiven. Any chance she got her mother made a point of belittling Zaheera's military accomplishments, or warning of danger to come. It was a wonder she'd never been seriously injured before, the way her mother went on about it. But in the end she'd been right. Zaheera thought about suggesting her mother take up a career as a fortune teller, then thought better of it. No need to play that game.

'At least the view is better than the book selection,' her mother said, staring out towards the field with the river at the bottom. 'Look, there's even a willow tree. Don't you just love willow trees? So majestic.'

'Mm hm,' Zaheera offered in response, not wanting to ruin her mother's observation by informing her that the willow tree was where she had found Jerry. This was the funny thing about death; it immediately removed certain topics or facts from conversation because to constantly point out something's relation to a death was to make everybody else uncomfortable. And so the one with the knowledge learned to bite one's tongue instead of sharing a point. This had been the way when she'd lost personnel before. There were soldiers she'd known who'd died in such horrific ways that to talk of their deaths was to either traumatise an unknowing individual, or open old wounds that those who did know would rather keep closed. And so everybody went along, removing more and more topics from conversation until there wasn't much more to say, leaving only silence. And silence was sometimes more painful than talking. There really was no winning with death. Zaheera wished there was some kind of manual for talking to people about the subject.

'Are they treating you well?' her mother asked.

'They are. Dr Griffiths and his staff have been very kind. They are patient and attentive, don't worry.'

'And you don't mind being shacked up in a room with boys?'

'It's no different in the barracks.'

'Yes, but there you have your own room.'

'And in the field?'

'Yes, well, that's different.'

'It's really not. I'm just lucky to have these facilities at my disposal. With any luck they'll have me back to full fitness and on my way in no time.'

'And what happens then?'

'Why do you ask?'

'Because Dr Griffiths informed me that you've handed in your resignation.'

'So much for doctor–patient confidentiality.' Zaheera berated herself for telling the doctor she'd decided to quit. This was exactly what she hadn't wanted to happen. Nothing would give her mother more pleasure than finding out Zaheera had decided to quit the military once and for all. The great and powerful Ameera Bhukari loved nothing more than to lord over her daughter, and finally witnessing her daughter quitting the military after years of hassling would be her crowning achievement.

'So what are you going to do now?'

'Serve out my notice.'

'Doing what?'

'Not my choice, really. I suppose they might move me to training new recruits or work off my last months in a recruiting office, or some other unimportant role.'

'No way they're putting a major in a recruitment office.'

'I don't really care at this point.'

'You should. They might send you back to the front line.'

'I'm fine with that, too.' She wasn't fine. This was absolutely the thing Zaheera felt deep within the core of her being that she no longer wanted to do. Anything but return to the front line. She was damned if she'd let her mother know, though.

'What if I offered you the chance to do something else for your remaining time in the military?'

'Offer? You're not in a position to offer me anything. You sell weapons for a living.'

'I design weapons for a living, amongst other things.'

'Same difference.'

'Not quite.'

'Whatever. You work for a private corporation that sells weapons to multiple national forces. What exactly could you offer that would require the specific services of one US military personnel? And who the hell would let you pick that person yourself?'

'That's what I came here to talk to you about.'

'What the hell does that mean?' Zaheera had assumed her mother was simply visiting because the doctor had said it was fine for her to check in on her daughter. She hadn't expected any ulterior motive.

Zaheera's mother stood facing the window, her back to Zaheera. She gazed out at the lawn, as if wondering where to start. 'Cappelli Technologies has been working on something quite advanced for the last few years. We're finally at a stage where we're ready for a field trial. Given that the project has been in large part funded by both the US and UK governments, we'll be looking to use soldiers from both forces for the test programme. Due to my part in the programme as chief designer, I have a little sway. I told them I had to have you on the team.'

'Why would you do that?'

'Because there's no soldier I know better in the world. And I don't know a better soldier. I can't imagine a more difficult test than getting your approval.'

'Approval on what?' Zaheera asked, choosing to ignore any general insinuation that came with her mother's statement.

'Well, you know we have the world's most advanced artificial intelligence solutions at Cappelli Technologies?'

'Yes.'

'Well, we've been working quite hard on combining our artificial intelligence with our advanced robotics solutions.'

'You have?'

'Yes. We've been working on designing the first completely AI soldier. It's a humanoid robot in design. Looks every part like your average grunt, as you say, except of course that it has no skin. It's just a kind of moving metal object that until recently was limited to basic functions like lifting and moving objects. However, the AI has come on in considerable leaps, and last year we had a breakthrough.

The breakthrough dramatically accelerated our design process.'

'What was the breakthrough?'

'In short, it was to do with the processing capabilities of the AI. Previously it was near perfect at pattern recognition and task execution. You could basically tell it to watch out for certain things and act in a certain way when specific things happened. But last year we managed to move the code on from pattern recognition to autonomous learning. The AI was suddenly able not only to learn whatever it was instructed to learn, but actually decide for itself what to learn. It started picking up on facts we hadn't told it and taking actions we hadn't prescribed.'

'You sure that's such a good thing?'

'Absolutely. We already have the AI conditioned to possess certain characteristics that we feel are crucial to human nature.'

'Such as shooting weapons at previously amicable people?'

'Don't be cute with me, young lady.'

Fuck me. Not 'young lady'. Anything but that fucking title.

'Anyway,' her mother went on, 'this momentous milestone resulted in a rapid increase in the AI's progression. It learned more over the next few days and became more sophisticated than we had managed since the inception of the project. Given that we've been working on robotics for just as long, and by then had a pretty solid working android, we decided to marry the two together and see what happened.'

'I'm sure your investors were thrilled.'

'What did I say about sassing me?'

'Sorry.'

'Forget about it. This is serious stuff, Zaheera. What we

have here is a functioning robot that can think for itself and act accordingly on the battlefield. It changes everything.'

She was right. Zaheera couldn't see how human soldiers had much of a future if robots were introduced to the mix. No sleep needed, no salaries, no pension plans, no PR disasters every time some pimple-faced teen got shot to shit on their first tour. 'How good is this machine at carrying out military duties?'

'That's what I want you to test.'

'What do you mean?'

'I want you to put them through their paces by way of a full military training exercise.'

'Them?'

'Yes. We've built a few models. And we've organised a programme to be carried out at a base in the Welsh hills usually used by the British forces. You'll lead the field operation, assisted at base by some British troops and potentially another few US troops. But predominantly I want you in the field with these things.'

'Why?'

'Because I want to know if you'd be willing to fight alongside one. If I convince you of the benefits, I can convince anybody. You're my litmus test, Zaheera. Your father raised a good soldier, the best. I know you'll test them properly, so when you come back saying how good they are, I'll know that we'll have taken the biggest step towards life preservation since the discovery of penicillin. Think about it – no more soldier deaths. No need to ever put somebody in needless danger. No human being need ever be sent to war again.'

'Sounds like a pipe dream to me. You'll always need somebody who can read a battlefield. There's no replacement for intuition. You might be able to put some fancy code in these things but they're not going to know what smoke smells like from a mile away, or when it's too quiet, so quiet that you know you're about to be ambushed. How's a computer going to decide whether it can stop a confrontation by talking to someone rather than putting a bullet in them because they're carrying a weapon? Those things can't be taught. You have to know.'

'Then prove it.'

'I'm not in the mood for your games. Dad wouldn't have approved of this nonsense.'

'Yeah, and where is your father now, huh? Had to always be the bloody hero and now he's gone. You got pretty damned close yourself. This is a good thing I'm working on, Zaheera. Think about it.'

'You can find your own way to reception. I need to get my head down.' Zaheera left the library without another word and went to her room to be alone.

5

The mood at Harley Manor that afternoon was a sombre one. By then Jerry's body had been removed from the premises and all his personal items had been collected from the room he had been staying in with Zaheera, Dave and Kendrick. His bed had been stripped and now stood empty, a silent gravestone-like marker for a grave none of them would ever see. Zaheera had successfully managed to avoid witnessing any of Jerry's family come to collect his personal items. She had no idea what they looked like nor how distraught they had been. For that she was grateful. Ashamed, but grateful.

She sat silently with her two remaining room-mates, each ruminating on the severity of war and the invisible wounds it inflicted upon the unwilling. Dr Griffiths had kindly offered to talk to each of them in turn if needed but all had declined. They wanted to be alone with their thoughts. It was how things got processed in the military: silently and severely. If needed, with alcohol. Harley Manor was what Dr Griffiths had noted as a dry campus. Even the kitchen was devoid of any alcoholic substances for cooking.

No sherry, no red wine, nothing. Despite storing a considerable amount of medicine at the manor, including some pretty strong pills that Zaheera had been told helped to numb oneself when needed, the doctor wasn't too keen on handing them out like candy.

And so the three of them sat in their room, keen to avoid any other human interaction, but keen also for a little something to make the pain go down a little easier.

'Fuck me, I'd kill for a pint,' Dave said, breaking the silence in the room. 'There's gotta be a pub somewhere round here.'

'We're not allowed to leave the manor,' Kendrick chimed in. 'Doctor's orders.'

'Fuck his orders.'

'You be willing to say that to his face?'

'Too right I would. Anyway, he's got other things to worry about. He's going to be up to his knickers in paperwork for the rest of the week. Let's get out of here.'

'There are plenty of other staff here to prevent us getting off the grounds.'

'Only if we try going out through the gate. They're not that strict about patrolling the perimeter. We could hop over the river and hoof it to the nearest village. Guarantee there'd be a pub. Every village in the UK has a pub. It's practically the law,' the bald-headed Scouse insisted. 'Come on,' he pleaded. 'First round's on me.'

Zaheera observed Kendrick, who seemed delighted to have someone as eager as himself to break out for a little bit. Dave was the ideal partner in crime: always up for a bit of mischief and ready to take the lead if needed. Kendrick smiled in mock acquiescence.

'What about you, Major?' Dave prodded. 'Fancy slumming it with us lowly bastards in Jerry's honour?'

Soldiers like him knew exactly how to get to an officer. Always making it a rank thing and then acting like the class divide was such that whatever was proposed was beneath an officer's standing. It almost always worked. At least, it worked on her. She wouldn't actually have needed much convincing. She was itching to get off the grounds and venture into civilisation. Anything to be away from white lab coats and feigned empathy. Were she back on base, she wouldn't be seen dead drinking with anybody other than an officer, but she figured the whole point here at Harley Manor, as Jerry had pointed out, was to do away with all the rank nonsense and simply try to heal alongside her fellow soldiers. The idea of sitting at a bar with a few grunts and drowning her sorrows was a welcome one. It would give her a chance to process not only Jerry's death, but also her team lost in Helmand and her mother's strange visit and subsequent offer. 'I'm in,' she said. 'Let's get out of here.'

The grins on both men's faces were wider than a twelve-year-old's possessing a stash of illegal fireworks. She grinned back as she hopped off her bed, feeling more energised than at any point since she had left Afghanistan.

THE TRIO SLIPPED out in the late afternoon, heading down to the river and sitting there quietly for about a half hour or so as a couple of groundsmen came and went. They waited until the coast was clear before quietly wading through the river. Zaheera took Dave's crutches across first, along with a rucksack with a chance of clothes for each one of the trio, then made her way back to assist Kendrick in hauling him through the waist-high water. They made a beeline for the hedge that ran the perimeter of the next field. It didn't provide a lot of cover, but it was enough in the now twilight hour to mask their escape.

Dave's prophecy of the village pub proved to be true. After an hour's walk through a number of fields, the group came over a dip into a small village with a stream running through it. Smack in the centre of town, adjacent to a small bridge crossing that Zaheera guessed could only allow one car over at a time, was a pub which, from their vantage point, looked to have a beer garden with a number of wooden benches out back. Each bench was already filled with occupants chatting with each other. From their distance, Zaheera could only make out a muffled murmur, with an occasional booming laugh from one rather animated old gent.

They made their way down the narrow country lane single file, sticking close to the hedge. The village itself was miniscule by anything Zaheera was familiar with. America simply didn't do quaint quite like the British. What constituted a small town back home still somehow seemed larger than this. This was barely worth naming. It was nothing more than a few houses and a pub. The high street, if it even merited the name, consisted primarily of a mini-supermarket, a newsagent, a coffee shop, and two different charity shops on either end of the street. The pub, then, appeared to be the only source of entertainment in this little countryside retreat. Upon closer inspection, the ancient and almost illegible sign hanging outside the pub read 'THE FOX AND HOUND'.

'Fucking hell,' Dave muttered, catching up with Zaheera and reading the sign. 'I could have bet you it would have some tosspot name like that. Woulda said Fox and Hound, or Queen's Arms, or the Crown. Any of that tosh. They're all the same. You familiar with the wonders of good British ale, Major?'

'I've dabbled,' Zaheera answered.

'Fantastic. These country pubs don't often do that mass-produced wank you get in the cities. This here's a good source of the real local stuff – the good stuff, the stuff that puts hairs on your chest and whatnot.'

'Just what I need,' she replied.

'Too right. Come on, then.' Dave led Zaheera and Kendrick into the pub.

Zaheera was only too happy to follow his lead. She wasn't entirely convinced anyone in the village looked like her or Kendrick. They might as well have gone around with flashing lights on their heads if they'd wanted less attention. The bustle of the pub died as soon as she and Kendrick stepped through the door, albeit momentarily, before everybody returned to their drinks. Not as hostile as first feared, then.

Inside, the pub proved to be as dark and dingy as every British pub Zaheera had ever entered in her life. That too seemed to be law. The wooden floor was packed with small dark wooden tables and chairs, each chair with some dark checked pattern on the cushions. In one corner, a small fire burned gently as an old ebony Labrador lay beside it, absorbing as much heat as it could while shedding much of its coat onto the floor. The bar too was a stained dark wood with an array of silver beer taps serving what looked to be predominantly lagers in the centre. Beside the taps, rubber drip trays with gawdy logos sat on the bar, full almost to the brim from various spillages throughout the evening so far. Further down the bar towards the end were a couple of brass cask ale taps with handwritten names where the logos would have been.

The barman, who looked like a carbon copy of Dave, equalling him in baldness, perhaps slightly more rotund, though, flipped a bar towel over his shoulder and leant on the handles of the two cask ales. 'All right, chaps,' he said to all three of them in what Zaheera recognised was a pretty strong cockney accent. 'What'll it be?'

'Which of the ales would you recommend?' Dave asked.

'Both bloody good by my standards, if you ask me. I should know. I brewed 'em. One's a pale ale, the other's your more traditional bitter. You 'ave a preference?'

'Pale ale's good for me,' Dave said.

'Me too,' Zaheera added.

Kendrick, clearly not wanting to be the odd one out, despite already being one of the two odd ones out, opted for the same choice. Pints eventually in hand, the three shimmied down the end of the bar opposite the fireplace with the resting Lab to keep away from the rest of the crowd.

'To Jerry,' Dave said, raising his glass.

'To Jerry,' Zaheera and Kendrick repeated. Zaheera took a long swig of the warm ale and thought of Jerry. She hadn't had a chance to find out what Jerry's battle had really been. Their meeting had been so brief, but he'd been kind and he'd made an effort to make her feel welcome at Harley Manor despite the obvious misery associated with one's being there as a result of some kind of requisite horrific physical or mental injury. Their conversation in the library had been an enjoyable one and it had helped Zaheera settle in – as far as that was possible – to Harley Manor. Had she been asked to speculate whether Jerry would attempt to take his own life again she'd have said no, regardless of his prior attempts. Despite his joke about being a risk, she had felt his admission of this made it less real, like somehow he had been over the worst of it.

She wondered what it was that had driven him to such depths.

She thought of her own guilt at having survived the attack on her convoy and the sickly feeling that sat in her stomach every minute of every day, unsure of how she was supposed to face the world knowing her team had all been gunned down. She being the only survivor somehow made it worse. Had anybody else made it, she might have had somebody to commiserate with, somebody to convince her it hadn't been her fault. This way there was no one. Somewhere out there in the desert she had lost many of the finest people she had known in her life. Johnson's bravery had been unlike anything she had witnessed before, and she considered herself somebody who had witnessed many brave actions from comrades throughout her military career, but the teenager's quick thinking and lack of hesitation was in all probability much of the reason she'd made it out. Had he not popped up on the gun and returned fire that quickly, they might have been overrun much sooner. Her mind replayed the image of his shooting as he twirled in the air and then slunk unceremoniously into the armoured vehicle below. It wasn't a fair death. He had been too young. Hell, most of them had been too young. But Johnson especially.

Rodriguez hadn't been as young, but his death hurt Zaheera just as much. She wondered how his wife and child were holding up. Probably not very well. Without Rodriguez abandoning his cover position and sprinting out into the night to save her, he might well have been the one to make it. Had her shitty rifle not jammed on her in the moment, everything might have been fine. For some reason the rifle had seemed like the right weapon to side with at the time. Something big and loud. A real spray-and-pray weapon that didn't require a whole lot of accuracy. In the moment, the pistol had suddenly felt lacking and she'd realised how quickly the encounter with the sniper could go wrong if her first shot had missed. It didn't matter now. The rifle had jammed and now everybody was dead except her. She had to live with that, somehow.

The trio sat in relative silence, each putting away pint after pint as their respective monsters traumatised them. Dave and Kendrick didn't look like they were faring any better than Zaheera, but there was some consolation at least in suffering together, sort of.

In the continued silence Zaheera thought of her mother's visit and the strange offer for her to work on a robotic soldier testing programme. The sheer arrogance of her mother to just assume that she would get her way infuriated Zaheera. Her mother knew how much being a soldier meant to Zaheera, indeed how much it had meant to her father before her, and yet here she was actively designing machinery that might one day remove the need for soldiers altogether. Zaheera was damned if she'd ever help bring about the downfall of human soldiers. You always needed soldiers. There was no replacement for human intuition in her mind. Besides, machines would be expensive. She couldn't imagine any time soon when a government would funnel enough resources into a military programme to replace entire human army with a bunch of machines.

She did, however, like the idea of being the one to prove that no machine could ever match a human soldier. That might wipe the smug look off her mother's face. Finally being the one to say she'd told her so would be a catharsis Zaheera could only dream of.

Her train of thought was interrupted by a couple of youngsters entering the pub. They couldn't have been much older than Johnson had been. Maybe eighteen or nineteen at most. One of them wore a flat cap positioned with the brim so far back on his head that his spiky fringe was untouched. He wore a maroon puffer jacket that drowned out his spindly frame. His mate was considerably bigger than him, requiring no puffer jacket to enhance his already rotund build. He wore a white polo shirt with the collar turned up and a big gold chain around his neck.

'Lads,' the barman said to them.

That answered Zaheera's question as to whether they were locals. The skinny one in the puffer jacket made his way confidently to the bar and ordered a pint of lager. The barman hesitated for a moment before doing as requested. Zaheera wondered whether his hesitation had been over their age or their look. People in a village like this probably knew each other quite well, she guessed, so the age thing was perhaps less likely. She figured that the barman's hesitation, then, was something to do with their behaviour. She met his eyes as he glanced over towards her before returning to his pouring and telling the lads, as he'd called them, that there might be a free table outside where they could park themselves for the night.

It didn't work.

Before Zaheera had a chance to turn her back to the two youths, the skinny one spotted her and his beady little eyes lit up like lights on Christmas tree.

'Well, 'ello, 'ello, 'ello. What 'ave we got 'ere, Gav? All the colours of the rainbow present tonight.'

The big one laughed. He didn't seem too forthcoming with the words, though. *Probably a little confusing for him.* Grunts and guffaws were more his bag.

'We've not seen youse lot round 'ere before, 'ave we, Gav?'

The big one shook his head. A big grin spread across his face. Zaheera could sense his excitement ratcheting up, like a dog knowing it was about to be taken out for a walk. His buddy was readying him for his treat.

'Just trying to enjoy a drink together in peace, thanks,' she replied.

'Ooh, we've got us a yank, Gav. A beautiful brown yank. What brings you to our little corner of the world, love?'

'The queues at Disney World were too long.'

The skinny one slapped his hand on the bar and laughed. 'Funny. You don't strike me as the Disney World type, if I'm being honest. Although, if you fancy a ride, I'm sure I could help out.'

'That's enough,' Dave said, squaring up to the kid.

'Who fucking asked you anything, cunt?'

The big one's grin grew wider, if that were possible. Zaheera sensed the situation getting out of hand quickly.

'Come on, Mike,' the barman said. 'Your dad's going to be in in no time. What would he say, hey?'

'You tell the inspector, if he gets here, to leave me the fuck alone.'

'Please,' Zaheera said, putting an arm on Dave's shoulder, 'we don't want any trouble. We're just trying to have a quiet drink together.'

The skinny one, Mike, looked over her shoulder at Kendrick sitting in the back. 'Fucking hell, mate. What happened to your face? Somebody try to beat the ugly out of you or something?'

Kendrick remained tight-lipped.

Dave moved even closer to young Mike, their foreheads practically touching.

Mike looked at the dagger tattoo on Dave's arm. 'Ah, Marine, hey. You lot a bunch of squaddies?'

'Come on,' Zaheera said to Dave and Kendrick, 'let's get out of here.' They held their ground silently for a moment, staring down the two troublemakers. Mike blew Dave a kiss but Dave didn't react. Good man. Zaheera led them out onto the street. They'd had their fun and now it was time to head back. Evidently the pub had been a bad idea. No surprise there. She breathed in the cool night air, glad to be shot of the situation. Most of her body was still in pain and the last thing she felt up to was a bar brawl.

They had barely made it to the end of the street when Zaheera heard Mike and Gav exit the pub behind them. 'Keep walking,' Zaheera muttered under her breath to her two companions.

'Oi, you lot,' Mike said, 'we weren't done with you.'

Zaheera kept walking in silence, listening intently as she heard the other two closing in on them. It didn't take long before they reached the edge of the miniscule town, away from cameras and potential witnesses. She stopped in her tracks, ignoring the instruction she had given to Dave and Kendrick. They were at a small junction between a few fields.

Mike and Gav were almost upon them. 'Fucking squaddies, hey, Gav? Always rolling around like they own the place. Why don't you lot just fuck off back to Afghanistan and leave our little town out of your pathetic wars.' He pulled out a lock blade from his back pocket and snapped it open.

In one swift move, Zaheera wrenched Dave back by the shoulder, out of reach of the open blade, and thrust her palm into Mike's face; he screamed in surprise. Gav growled like a terrier and piled in with his fists. She blocked the first two but the third landed square in her stomach and keeled her over, the pain from her bullet wounds still evident, not that she needed an additional excuse to keel over at the power of his blow.

She looked around and saw Dave and Kendrick take on Gav, the enormous teen absorbing many of their blows as if they were a minor nuisance.

Mike had just about recovered from the blow to his face and attacked Zaheera with the lock blade. She dodged once as he slashed at her, grabbed the knife-wielding wrist with one hand and delivered a blow to his neck with her other elbow. He went down like a sack of shit, clutching at his throat and gasping for breath.

Behind her she heard what she presumed was Gav being thrown into a ditch on the side of the road.

'You boys had enough?' she said. Gav grumbled something from down in the ditch while Mike rolled on the road in front of her. They were done. 'Come on,' she said to Dave and Kendrick. 'Might be best if we get the hell out of Dodge.'

6

They left the two troublemakers where they lay on the road and in the ditch respectively and hotfooted it back the way they had come towards Harley Manor. Zaheera had been in enough fights to know that sticking around didn't really help matters. She didn't want Dave and Kendrick getting into any unnecessary trouble. Of course there was no guarantee that Mike and Gav wouldn't report their injuries, but her guess was that they had been embarrassed enough and would not be looking to get their beating officially recorded in writing. That had been her experience with these kinds of people. Usually the cuts and bruises were enough of a reminder not to go seeking additional trouble. Reporting things to the police encouraged investigation into both sides of the story and that usually put everybody on shaky ground.

The body shot she'd taken from big Gav still ached. She caressed the bruised area at the top of her stomach, careful not to press too hard, especially over her bottom rib, which she was growing increasingly concerned might actually have sustained a minor fracture. The bastard had really socked it to her. Even breathing was a painful ordeal. Still, in comparison to the other two she looked great. Big Gav had really gone to town on them.

Dave, the one-legged Marine, had taken a blow to the nose and was developing some pretty convincing panda eyes as the bruises set in. The nose itself looked terrible. A patch of red highlighted where Gav's hit had taken much of Dave's skin clean off, and both his nostrils were filled with some tissue he'd pulled from his pocket to stop the bleeding. Dave's hands were a mess, with both fists visibly swollen and bleeding from their earlier exertion. Still, you had to give it to the guy. He was still getting over his recent loss of limb and wasn't exactly what one would call confident on his crutches, but he'd been the first to step up to the fight and hadn't backed down an inch when taking on one of the biggest thugs Zaheera had seen on Civvy Street, as she knew he'd call it.

Kendrick's face somehow managed to look worse, despite his burn wounds providing a fairly horrific base. He had what Dave had lovingly called an 'egg' on his forehead above one eye where the swelling from a punch had set in. As a result that eye wouldn't open, leaving him with one remaining barely functioning bloodshot eye. He hadn't said much the whole evening. Hell, he hadn't said much since Zaheera had met him. She was starting to like that about him; no need to say anything unless he had something of value to add. People like that were a rare treat in her world, regardless of her rank theoretically conditioning others not to speak too freely in her presence.

It took them a lot longer to make it back to Harley Manor than it had taken to get out. Dave was slower on his crutches. He hadn't complained once but Zaheera could see from the occasional wince and his reduced speed that it had taken a lot out of him. The tough bastard wouldn't stop when she offered him a chance to relax. She liked him more with every step and decided she would have been proud to have had him on her team in battle. Kendrick, too. His silent determination earned him a place in Zaheera's usually impossible to please heart.

Their arrival back at Harley Manor did not go as Zaheera had hoped. They found staff searching the grounds with torches and Dr Griffiths seething in reception. It was impossible for them to sneak by.

'Really?' Dr Griffiths said. 'After everything we've just been through with Jerry, you fucking idiots think it's fine to disappear on me like that? What the hell were you thinking?' He called for a nurse to come and attend to their injuries. 'Please tell me I don't need to go looking for civilian bodies anywhere.'

'You don't,' Zaheera said. 'They'll be fine. Just a misunderstanding.'

'I think the misunderstanding was between you and I, Zaheera. I had mistaken you for a respectable officer, not some lout looking for a fight.'

'We weren't looking for a fight. We just needed a taste of normality. Jerry's death hit us too, you know.'

'Save it. I've called your mother. She'll be here any minute now.'

Shit. 'What did you do that for?'

'Had to check if she'd seen you, didn't I? I hadn't expected you to go to her, but then I also hadn't expected you to start picking fights with the locals.' He paced back and forth in front of them as a nurse bandaged Zaheera's knuckles. 'I can barely stand the sight of you right now. You could have given me a heart attack.'

'I'm sorry.'

'Get out of my sight.'

'I swear, Zaheera, I'm convinced you do these things to punish me, but for the life of me I do not know why.'

'I'm sorry, Mom,' Zaheera, feeling belittled, responded in front of Dave and Kendrick, who chuckled.

'Don't *sorry* me, my dear. Get in the car before I change my mind and drive home alone.'

Dr Griffiths shook her mother's hand and then left them to it. Zaheera, it seemed, would be allowed to spend the night in her mother's care, provided she returned at the crack of dawn the next day. Her mother had assured Dr Griffiths that would indeed be the case, and that she felt a good talk with her daughter was exactly what the situation had called for. The doctor agreed.

Zaheera got into the passenger seat of her mother's coupé and rested her head on the window so as not to encourage any unwanted conversation. She was not in the mood for a motherly lecture. Civvy Street, as Dave called it, could be such a nightmare sometimes. This hadn't been the first fight Zaheera had been involved in when returning from a tour of duty. No matter what the national sentiment had been towards whichever military conflict she'd been involved in, there was always some civilian who delighted in picking a fight with recently returned soldiers. Previous returns to New York had been just as bad. It was why she found drinking alone at home to be easier. Less enjoyable, but easier. At least there was some relief in the knowledge that there were assholes in England just the way there were in America. She recalled the previous tour she'd returned from a couple of years ago, where she'd headed to a rooftop bar in Brooklyn and had parked herself in the corner, minding her own business. A couple of young guys, real bro-dudes, one of whom seemed utterly thrilled with himself for wearing his cap backwards, had upbraided her for not being cheerful enough and had then told her just how much things would improve if she wasn't such a bitch. They'd followed her most of the way home until she led them into an alleyway and taught them both a lesson they wouldn't soon forget. The one who'd called her a bitch had apologised profusely after Zaheera had bounced his head off the ground a few times. She'd left them there lying in their own blood to ponder over their actions. Civilians and soldiers did not mix well when alcohol was involved, in her opinion. She'd seen it enough times with men getting defensive when her fellow male officers walked into clubs with her, shirts wrapped around their muscular torsos like Saran wrap. It was always the same story: the girls' heads turned and their boyfriends got mad. The soldiers, fresh from months of fear and frustration, were keen to let loose. Inevitably some inebriated civilian fool's jealousy would boil over and he would decide to pick a fight with one of the soldiers and the night would take an ugly turn. It made her pine for the simplicity of Afghanistan. Just her team and the mission in hand. And a whole lot of desert.

'You know you can talk to me,' her mother said as the car hurtled through the night. 'We don't always have to do the silent treatment thing.'

'I know.'

'Wow, two whole words. I should throw a parade.'

'Suit yourself.'

'Oh, come off it, Zaheera. You're not sixteen anymore. I came to get you, didn't I?'

'Sure.'

'Right, well, let's count that as one in my favour for once.'

'Are we still counting that against you leaving home for another country after Dad died, just so you wouldn't have to be burdened with me?'

'Enough. Firstly, America might have been your home, but it wasn't to me or your father.'

'Yes it was. Dad fought for America.'

'He was grateful. He wanted to give back. Look what that got him.'

'Ugh.' Zaheera turned once more towards the window and watched the street lights pass by overhead one by one. 'How long until we get back to yours?' she snapped.

'We're not going back to mine.'

'What?'

'I have something I want to show you.'

ZAHEERA'S MOTHER drove another couple hours in relative silence towards the outskirts of London. Zaheera had never visited her mother's office before and hadn't a clue what to expect. Still, given that she worked for the biggest technology company in the world, leading the way in artificial intelligence development and military engineering, it was hard not to be unimpressed when they eventually entered the parking lot of her mother's office. The South London building looked from the street almost like an abandoned office block, with many boarded-over windows and cheap grey pebbledash coating on the outer walls.

The street-level car park eventually gave way to an underground entrance, which Zaheera's mother drove into with a grin. 'Don't judge a book by its cover.'

'Hard not to when the cover's in tatters.'

'It's intentional.'

'Your HQ is intentionally shit?'

'It's not the headquarters. It's where my division is based. And given the nature of our work, we quite like the less showy exterior. Keeps the undesirables away.'

Zaheera wasn't sure whether by undesirables she meant journalists, board members or the public but decided not to ask. It was one of those annoyingly self-congratulatory phrases, delivered in such a way as to invite another question. *Just fucking say what you have to say.*

Once underground, the car park lit up like a stadium. Zaheera's mother parked up and led her to the lift, which took them up to her office on the fourth and top floor.

'So what is it you want to show me?'

'Patience. You're just like he was, you know.'

'I know.' Zaheera's guard softened slightly as she smiled at the memory of her father, always so keen to be on the move, to conquer whatever needed conquering.

Other than the security guard they'd passed driving onto the premises, the building was empty. The lights were all off and the building gave Zaheera vibes of a mall job she'd had in her teens. She'd hated opening the coffee shop in the mornings. The dark unpopulated mall had always made her uncomfortable. It reminded her of post-apocalyptic novels she'd read at the time that were forever setting themselves in abandoned malls and other such locations. This building was no better. She felt the hairs on the back of her neck rise and slowed her breathing, ready for the monster to show itself.

Her mother, oblivious to Zaheera's childhood trauma, whistled as she walked over to one wall and looked into a retina scanner, which promptly allowed her to turn all the lights on.

Zaheera's eyes were instantly drawn to the centre of the floor. Between all the desk pods was an open circular space.

Something almost human in shape was in the centre. At first Zaheera thought it was a mannequin, like the ones she'd seen in the mall as a kid before they got all dressed up in whatever fast fashion was being peddled that week. Upon closer inspection she realised it was something much more technical. It was presumably one of the humanoid robots her mother had been talking about. The bot was standing up but with shoulders sagged and head bowed. It didn't appear to be turned on.

'Zaheera, I want you to meet Alpha.'

Upon hearing its name the bot came to life. It straightened its stance and looked at the two Bhukari women. 'Good evening, Ameera.'

It fucking talks!

Zaheera knew that artificial intelligence was plenty advanced and businesses had been using chatbots as software for years, but something about the voice coming from a two-metre tall android made her a little queasy.

'Who is your friend?' Alpha asked.

'This is my daughter, Alpha. Her name is Zaheera.'

'It is a pleasure to meet you, Zaheera.' The bot proffered its hand. 'Your mother and I know each other very well. I would go so far as to say we are friends, wouldn't you, Ameera?'

'Yes, Alpha. We are friends.'

Zaheera stood nonplussed shaking the bot's hand. It lacked any real human appearance, what with it having a hard metallic frame. Its facial features were non-existent, save for one white horizontal LED light for its eyes and a speaker for its mouth. Still, it looked more advanced than anything Zaheera had ever set eyes on. She assumed the lack of human likeness was intentional. Knowing her mother, she'd have given it everything from eyelashes and rosy cheeks if she felt it necessary. No, this thing was built for purpose. Lean and neutral-looking, Zaheera guessed so that no one country would be put off buying multiple shipments of these for their militaries.

'What exactly can you do?' she asked it.

'I'm not sure I understand the question,' Alpha responded.

'Great start,' she replied.

'Alpha,' her mother cut in, 'is designed to do whatever is needed. He's more intelligent and more athletic than any human soldier out there. He doesn't get tired and if he ever gets wounded, we can simply replace the damaged parts and get him going again. He is the future.' She beamed.

'Looks like he'd be better off stacking shelves than fighting wars.'

'Brave words from someone who hasn't seen him in motion. You think he's so crap, why don't you try him?'

'Try what, exactly?'

'Do your worst. Try take him out.'

That got her attention. This lump of scrap metal couldn't really be better than a soldier. She cocked her head and checked its musculature. It appeared to be made up of all sorts of wires and cogs, cased in a hard shell. 'You ever pulled the back off a TV?' she asked Alpha.

'I have not yet had that privilege.'

'It's a clusterfuck of cabling. That's what you look like underneath that armour. How the hell are you going to survive in water or sandy deserts, hey?'

'I am designed to keep most debris out and any that does make it through my armour can be cleaned with ease.'

'Enough chit-chat,' her mother said. 'Are you going to take him on or not?'

Zaheera still couldn't make her mind up. The last thing she wanted was to be drawn into one of her mother's games.

'You don't have to if you fear me,' the bot said.

Mistake.

'Non-lethal, if you wouldn't mind, Alpha,' her mother said as Zaheera stepped up.

'Affirmative,' the bot responded. It too took up a ready stance, placing its feet shoulder width apart and raising its fists like a boxer.

Zaheera, conscious of the wounds she still carried, knew she would not be on her best form. The bot's provocation, however, was inadmissible. She'd need to be quick. She went straight for its ankles, trying to tip the thing over. Alpha reacted in a flash, nimbly stepping back to avoid her strike and then countering with a blow that sent her spiralling to the floor.

'Is that it?' the bot asked.

Zaheera wiped a slick of blood from her bottom lip and spat on the ground. Her tongue swelled inside her mouth where she had bitten down on its edge, which had hurt more than the blow from the bot. 'You're funny. We usually beat that out of soldiers the first week of training.' She got to her feet, trying to hide their jelly-like stability, and flicked her plait over her shoulder. 'Come on, then.'

Alpha came for her this time. It led with its right but Zaheera saw it in time, parrying the blow and countering with her knee. The bot was fast, though. Faster than anyone she had ever fought. It parried and countered everything she threw at it and made it look like it was just warming up. She tried switching fighting styles but that didn't matter either. A flurry of punches and a deadly right hook later and she was back down on the ground, her ears ringing and her eyes seeing stars. Somewhere behind her she heard her mother's voice but it was indecipherable. It sounded like the low warble of a radio slightly out of tune.

She ignored the voice and got back to her feet, cricking her neck side to side. This thing clearly had all the official martial arts styles encoded. It hadn't grown up in Brooklyn, though. There was no manual for New York street fighting. She ran at it, arms and legs flailing, not really knowing herself which limb she'd thrust first. In the end she went with her knee, followed by both hands slapping either side of the bot's face at the same time. Its little LED screen stuttered for a second. *Seems a blow to the head is a blow to the head, regardless of what you're made of.*

It staggered back a couple of steps.

This is it. Go for the kill.

She charged, her shoulder down, ready to clothesline it.

Whether it had faked the injury or not, she wasn't sure, but as she got near it, the bot straightened up and back-handed her like she was no more than a fly being swatted. She fell to the ground for the third and final time, her vision now so blurred she couldn't make out the stars from the explosions in front of her eyes.

The bot dived on top of her and held her in a grapple until whatever remaining dignity she had was gone. And just like that, it was over. She hadn't stood a chance.

Eventually her mother instructed the bot to let her go.

Zaheera stood up and walked back to the door. She'd seen enough. The shock had firmly set in. 'Take me back to Harley Manor.'

7

I t was morning by the time she returned to Harley Manor and following another stern talking to from Dr Griffiths about what constituted acceptable behaviour from an officer, she'd been informed that she, Dave and Kendrick were fine to continue their stay at Harley Manor for now. The military, as ever, was keen not to lose out on its investment, she figured.

After telling her off and warning her never to leave the grounds again without his permission, Dr Griffiths informed Zaheera that some of the families of her recently deceased comrades had been flown to the UK for a holiday following a charitable donation intended to give grieving families some respite from the horrors they were now having to face up to. Dr Griffiths had been given permission to inform Zaheera of the various families who'd accepted the trip, one of whom turned out to be Rodriguez's wife and kid. She'd never met them but felt very much like she knew them well, given how often he'd gone on about them. Dr Griffiths offered to call them on her behalf and ask if they'd want to see her. She was touched by his sincerity and the speed at which he'd gone from authoritarian schoolteacher to loving parent. She accepted his offer, knowing that she had to see them to pay her respects. Rodriguez would have done the same for her, she knew.

Zaheera rested her eyes that morning and when she awoke, she found that a taxi had been called for her. All the way back to London the butterflies in her stomach prevented a single moment's sanity. As yet, she hadn't spoken to anybody who had known her team. Somehow she was more apprehensive about seeing them than she had been about facing doctors, nurses or shrinks. None of them actually *knew*. These people would *know*. Their pain would be real. As real as her own. She resented her own survival even more in that moment.

The driver informed Zaheera that he was taking her to Richmond, an idyllic district in South West London which, he noted, housed a famous park populated with the King's deer. It sounded like a nice place for a break from life. She hoped Rodriguez's wife and kid were enjoying it as much as one could in such a circumstance.

The taxi pulled up outside a hotel on Richmond Hill a couple of hours later. Zaheera's breath caught momentarily as she admired the view of the surrounding forest and gentle dip of green fields down to the Thames. It was a world apart from the dingy South London location she'd been to the night before when visiting her mother's office. She thanked the driver and made her way to the hotel reception where she was told that Adriana Rodriguez and her daughter Gloria were expecting her. They were sitting in the café enjoying tea and scones as Zaheera entered. She was taken by Adriana's beauty. It was almost impossible to think of her as a mother. She didn't look a day over twenty as she sat there in a white summer dress and Roman sandals, her luscious hair falling in dark, graceful curls over her shoulders. She was effortless beauty personified. *Rodriguez did well for himself. No wonder he never showed us any pictures; the guys would have had a field day.*

Opposite the beautiful Adriana sat the cutest little girl Zaheera had ever laid eyes on. Every bit her mother's daughter, with olive skin and similarly dark hair, albeit not quite as well taken care of, but with mischievous little eyes that Zaheera realised were her father's. Her cheeks were caked with clotted cream and strawberry jam as she giggled to her heart's content, blissfully ignorant of the anguish in her mother's expression as she was watched over.

Zaheera pushed the urge to leave out of her mind and walked over to the table. 'Mrs Rodriguez?'

'Yes?'

'I'm Zaheera Bhukari. It's a pleasure to meet you.'

Adriana Rodriguez stood at once, looking suddenly on edge and her eyes quickly welling up. She shook Zaheera's hand. 'Thank you for coming. It's very kind of you.'

'Not at all. Thank you for seeing me.' Zaheera looked about the café. A few other tables were occupied and within eavesdropping distance. 'Shall we take a walk outside?' she asked. 'It would be a shame not to take advantage of such a beautiful day.'

Adriana, clearly grateful to Zaheera for the suggestion as she pulled a pack of tissues from her handbag and extracted one in preparation for their conversation, enthusiastically agreed to the idea. 'Come on, Gloria. We're going to take a walk with Major Bhukari.'

'How did you know my rank?'

'Please,' she tutted. 'Arturo talked about you all the time.'

It took Zaheera a moment to remember that Arturo had

been Rodriguez's first name. She couldn't recall the last time someone had addressed him as Arturo. 'All good, I hope?'

'Of course. He adored you. Would have done anything for you.'

Now it was Zaheera's turn to blink away the tears before she made a mess of herself. They walked out of the hotel and down a long gravel path that led eventually to the river at the bottom. The sun hung overhead, and little Gloria skipped in front of Zaheera and Adriana walking side by side, trying unsuccessfully to catch a pair of butterflies obsessing with one another in the long grass. Zaheera thought of the conversation she'd had with Rodriguez and Johnson in the armoured vehicle before everything went to shit about their ideas for R and R. Johnson's quip about Rodriguez spending all his time on diaper duty was a little out of date, it seemed.

'She's bigger than I expected,' Zaheera said, not knowing any better way to break the silence between herself and Adriana.

'And growing by the day,' Adriana replied affectionately. 'Gloria, stick to the path,' she gently scolded the little girl as her pursuit of the pair of butterflies took her further and further from her mother.

'Okay, Mom,' she replied, before running deeper into the grass after the butterflies, giggling with delight.

'Just like her father,' Adriana said. 'Never paid attention.' Her lip quivered as she fought back a sob.

'How did the two of you meet?' Zaheera asked.

'In a bar in San Diego,' she replied. The memory brought a smile to her face and returned some of the radiance Zaheera had noticed earlier. 'He had recently passed training and was celebrating with some friends. He was beautiful. You should have seen him then. His smile was disarming, and his cool, calm nature made me want to spend the whole night talking to him. I loved talking to him. On subsequent nights I would lie on his chest listening to him talk about our future plans. He was such a dreamer. It didn't take much to be swept away when you spoke to him. In his presence I felt like I was always on some drug, something warm and sweet that sat in your belly and made you content, you know?'

'I don't, but I wish I did,' Zaheera said.

'I'm sorry to hear that. Well, with him it was a haze of ambition. Every year some new goal, some new adventure we were going to go on. And he kept his word, mostly. Military life has a way of obstructing certain options, you know.'

'Only too well.'

'We were saving up to move before—' She wiped a stray tear from one cheek.

'Before all this?' Zaheera offered.

'Yes. Before *this*. We were going to leave America and come to Europe. Arturo wanted to open a café near the sea. He said we could live above it and work the shop together during the days, just him and me, while Gloria was at school, and in the evenings we could sit and look out at the Mediterranean as we shared book recommendations with each other. Or we could go for long walks with Gloria. He said she'd love it, what with Italy practically having a gelato shop on every corner.'

'That sounds like a wonderful dream.'

'It was. I was going to business school at night while he was on tour. I wanted to be ready to run the business with him, to make sure it was a success. I'd look after Gloria during the day and then leave her at my mother's in the evening whilst I went and studied. It helped with the loneliness, too.'

'I'm sure it did,' Zaheera said. 'I've never envied military spouses. We are so lucky in the military – we have each other. The camaraderie is what gets us through most of it. I can't imagine what it's like to be the one at home waiting for months at a time.'

'It was awful, but I did it for him.'

'He was a lucky man.'

'I was the lucky one,' Adriana said.

They walked in silence for a few minutes, lapping up the sun on their backs and stopping to smell the occasional flower in amongst the grass. Gloria continued to gallop around them with seemingly unlimited energy. Having reached the river, they took the gravel path alongside it leading away from Richmond. On the water a couple in a rowing boat passed alongside them, too besotted with each other to take much notice. Zaheera thought about the Rodriguez' dream of moving to Italy. It was a good one. She hadn't considered that Rodriguez was planning on leaving the military. It made his sacrifice all the more painful to bear, realising what he had knowingly given up to come save her out in that rocky outcrop. Now she had to live with that guilt, too. Adriana and Gloria would almost certainly never leave America now, their dreams and their world shattered. Little Gloria would not get to spend her days eating gelato or going for long walks with her mother and father. Instead Gloria would now have to grow up without her father. Zaheera was grateful in that moment that she had at least known her own father for most of her life. She'd been almost ready to graduate when he had died. At the time she had cursed the world for taking him from her. The loss had almost broken her. Only now did she realise how lucky she had been to have had him in her life for as long as she did. He got to see her grow up. He knew she was going to follow him into the military. She had been able to learn from him and seek his advice when needed, or seek comfort when advice wouldn't do. Gloria would have none of that.

'What was he like?' Adriana eventually asked as they rounded a bend in the river.

'What do you mean?'

'You know, in the military. I only knew him at home. What was he like with you all?'

'He was brilliant,' Zaheera said. 'One of the finest soldiers I ever had the honour of serving with.' She knew she'd have said that anyway. Indeed she had said it to many families before, but it helped that on this occasion she really meant it. He really had been one of the finest. 'He used to tell us all about the little family he had back home and how we should all hurry up and start with marriage and kids. We all said he was mad. Never showed us a picture of you, though. It's clear now why he didn't.'

Adriana blushed a little and smiled.

'As I was saying, any time we were stuck chatting, Rodriguez – sorry, Arturo – would wax lyrical about family life being the best thing in the world. Had me half convinced about settling down eventually.'

'It's nice to hear he talked about us,' Adriana said. 'And he was a good soldier?'

'Like I said, one of the best. One of the only people I knew who could drive an armoured vehicle like it was a go-kart on a track. It was like he was a part of the vehicle. He understood them. Same thing when it came to weapons, too. He was a dab hand on the gun range.' Zaheera paused as Gloria came up and pulled on her mother's dress to complain she was tired and that they should stop. They sat on a low wall looking at the river, Gloria on her mother's lap, curled into her chest. She was asleep almost instantly. The water lapped against the edge of the riverbank and birds perched on the canvas yacht canopies, most of which were stained white from all the previous droppings. 'He was a messy sonofabitch, though,' Zaheera went on. 'Never met someone who was such a nightmare to keep in check.'

Adriana laughed. 'He was the same at home.'

'Yes, well, it was infuriating for his superiors. We all had to think of more and more inventive ways to punish him in the hope he'd get his shit together. I once got his whole platoon up during a rainstorm one night. None of 'em were thrilled about it. They got marched out onto the parade square where I put Arturo in the middle and made them all run in circles around him with their rifles above their heads while he did nothing. Made them all shout, "Thank you, Corporal Rodriguez," while they were at it.'

'I bet they loved him for that,' Adriana said, wiping a cheerful tear from her cheek.

'They did. They all loved him. I heard they might have taken it in turns getting him up to scratch with keeping his gear squared away after the parade square incident, though.'

'I'm sure.'

Gloria woke and listened intently as Zaheera continued to regale them with humorous anecdotes about Rodriguez's various failings. It wasn't long before all three were laughing with tear-filled eyes. Zaheera told some stories just for Gloria, who loved hearing about her father, and giggled each time Zaheera landed the punchline of each anecdote. Gloria never asked any questions, though. She laughed and then she cried. And then Zaheera and Adriana cried with her. Somewhere, amongst all the tears, the three of them found a catharsis in the sharing of stories. They talked all afternoon and into the evening until the sun started to set; all the while Adriana apologised to Zaheera, telling her she was more than welcome to leave, and Zaheera professed that there was nowhere she'd rather be. She meant it, too. Eventually, after hearing a couple of foxes come barking somewhere nearby, they decided to head back before it got too late.

Adriana encouraged Gloria to run on ahead as they walked back up the hill towards the hotel before turning once more to Zaheera. 'He didn't die in pain, did he?' she asked.

'No,' Zaheera confirmed, knowing that this question had probably been on her mind all afternoon. 'It was quick. He saved my life in the process.'

'What happened?'

'How much have you been told?'

'Just that he was part of a convoy that was attacked and eventually overrun.'

'It was much more than that. The whole thing would have been over in a matter of seconds if it hadn't been for Arturo and a few others. We were pinned down for hours. We thought we'd almost got them all but there was this one sniper that we couldn't get to. Arturo and I were the last two remaining by this point. We waited until the cover of night and then I crept out into the dark to take out the sniper whilst Arturo kept watch from the vehicles. I told him to stay put.' By now tears were streaming down Zaheera's face again. This time it didn't feel cathartic. She was ashamed. Ashamed for not being good enough to take the sniper out herself. Ashamed that Rodriguez had to come out and save her. 'It's my fault,' she managed after choking back a sob.

'No,' Adriana said. 'No it's not. I know my Arturo. There was no way he'd have left someone out there on their own.'

'You're right about that. I eventually came upon the sniper but my weapon jammed. Had Arturo not come bounding over the rocks at that very moment the sniper would have killed me. Instead he got Arturo. It was quick. The sniper died soon after.' Zaheera stopped in her tracks, utterly defeated, and Adriana wrapped her up in a strong embrace. 'I'm so sorry, Adriana.'

'Don't be,' she said. 'I'm proud of him. I'm glad he was with you at the end.'

ZAHEERA ARRIVED BACK at Harley Manor late that night and put herself straight to bed. She barely said a word to her room-mates or any of the staff. She wanted to be left alone. The day had been too much. Self-pity didn't seem fair when Adriana and Gloria now had to figure out a life without Rodriguez, but Zaheera couldn't help but dwell on her own pain, either. She'd lost people before but never on such a scale. The price was too high. Sleep evaded her for hours as she relived the convoy attack over and over again, wondering about the families and loved ones of the other fallen. How many other Glorias and Adrianas were there? How many lives irrevocably broken in one afternoon?

She messaged her mother and asked to speak to her the next day before rolling over and putting her head under her pillow.

Sleep eventually came for Zaheera, along with the monsters.

8

Zaheera caught up with Dave and Kendrick at breakfast the next morning. They too had received another telling off from Dr Griffiths, Dave informed her, but no other punishment followed. Instead they intended to keep their heads down and build back a bit of trust with the good doctor.

They asked how Zaheera's visit to Rodriguez's wife and kid had gone and Zaheera, sparing them the vast majority of the details, informed them that it had been a tough visit but a good one for all parties involved.

'Poor bird,' Dave said. 'All on her bill now, looking after the little 'un.'

'She'll figure out a way,' Kendrick said. 'They all do eventually.'

One of the nurses came over to their table and informed Zaheera that her mother had arrived and was waiting in the library for her. Zaheera hadn't expected her so early in the morning but found herself somewhat touched by her mother's immediate response to her message the night before. She thanked the nurse and excused herself from the table.

'Thanks for coming so quickly,' she said to her mother as she entered the library. Mother and daughter hugged each other firmly and Zaheera felt whatever animosity had been bubbling up of late wash away. Her mother was here out of genuine concern, she could see that now, and she was grateful for it.

'Of course,' her mother said. 'Anything for you.'

'You really mean that, don't you?'

'With every fibre of my being.'

'Thanks, Mom.' She took one of her mother's hands and massaged it gently. 'Do you ever miss Dad?'

'What kind of question is that?'

'I don't mean do you remember him, or is life any different without him – I mean do you *miss* him?'

'Every day. I might still be mad at him for always going off to fight other people's wars, but that man was my world. Before you, he was everything to me.'

'I miss him too,' Zaheera said. 'I met the wife and child of one of my old team yesterday. He'd been killed during the attack on the convoy. The only reason I'm still standing here is because of him.'

'How was it, seeing them?'

'Tough. It always is, but you do it as much for yourself as for them. Sometimes it's just nice to commiserate with somebody who knew your friend, you know?'

'I do.'

'Well, the little girl couldn't have been much older than three. She was tiny. Such a fun little thing. And now she's going to grow up in a world with no father. I used to curse the world for being so cruel to me by taking Dad away from me, but yesterday I felt lucky to have had as much time with him as I did. This little girl has nothing.'

'It was always one of my fears,' her mother said. 'I didn't

want you to grow up without a father. I didn't want to live without a husband, either. That little girl has a long and tough road ahead of her.'

'She does,' Zaheera agreed. 'His wife, too, has lost everything before their lives had even really got going. How do you move on without the person you've built your life with?'

'With great difficulty.'

Zaheera nodded, acknowledging the struggle her mother had been through. She realised how often their conversations had been about whether she, Zaheera, was doing all right, but not as much how her mother was doing. She wanted to go to her mother and hug her again, but their relationship was only just beginning to mend. They weren't back to levels of familiarity where hugs could just be handed out and received at random. There was an element of time that had to be put in again. All these years her mother had been living and working in the UK while Zaheera had remained stationed in America or on tour in various inhospitable countries. It started to dawn on her just how much her mother had needed to change up her scenery to help her move on. Zaheera was lucky enough to have had the military do that for her. Her mother, on the other hand, would have been haunted by the same house, the same streets, the same life being lived without its key ingredient. She realised that now. Her mother's work on this artificial soldier programme made a lot more sense to her. Suddenly she was more curious to understand it. 'Tell me about this programme you want me on, then.'

'I'm so glad you asked. Like I said before, we've been simultaneously working on artificial intelligence and humanoid robotic design. The design of these robots is great. They're fast, nimble and durable. Physically, I have utmost faith in their ability to keep up to speed with a human soldier. I still want that confirmed by rigorous testing, but I believe we've designed something solid. It was the AI that really impressed me over the last year, though. The advances have been incredible. They're not just computers anymore, Zaheera. I'm talking genuine intelligence. I almost feel we need to name it something other than AI – that term insults what they are.'

'Okay. You have my attention. Where do I fit in?'

Her mother smiled. 'I want you to put them through their paces. You are the best judge of character I know. You take them out into the field and you test them, same way you would test any soldier, except there can't be any room for the benefit of doubt. There's too much riding on this. I would rather you fail them and we go back to the drawing board than somebody else pass them and we put ineffective bots into the armed forces.'

'Do you think I'll fail them?'

'I think you'll try very hard to.'

'That's not an answer.'

'No. I don't think you will.'

'And why is that?'

'Because they passed *my* tests,' her mother said. 'And the only person who holds standards more ridiculous than yourself is the person who taught you those standards.'

She had a point. Zaheera had figured that her mother would have already put all of these bots through some kind of wringer. The same woman who had her doing practice tests for the year ahead during the summers before each school year kicked off would certainly leave no stone unturned. No, these androids would have been thoroughly examined. She couldn't make up her mind whether it comforted her to know that these bots were competently designed or whether it disturbed her to know that they were clearly so good it was now worth considering them replacements for real soldiers. Still, if it meant that future little Glorias might never have to go through life without a father then it was worth finding out. 'Okay,' she said. 'Suppose I'm interested. What kind of testing are we talking about? Are we doing it here in the UK?'

'Yes.' Her mother put one of the library books she had been perusing back on the shelf. 'There's a military training camp in Wales that's used by some of the more specialist British forces. It's out of the way and it will be minimally staffed. It'll be free from cameras and media speculation. We just want to see whether these things work or not. The training camp is pretty basic, but it has enough of the usual requirements. There's an obstacle course to test their agility, a firing range to test their prowess with weapons, and then there's the location itself among the Welsh valleys, with thousands of acres of wild land to really put them through their paces. They need to pass an endurance march. Then once you've put them through all the basic tests, I want you to do a full field test.'

'How full?'

'Similar to that SERE training you did.'

This was more than Zaheera was expecting. The Survival, Evasion, Resistance and Escape course was a high-level training programme taught by US armed forces and adopted by the UK's SAS and SBS, which trained military personnel to evade capture and survive in hostile environments, as well as dealing with interrogation techniques. It made sense when she thought about it, but it was an extreme option. Even she hadn't thought of putting them through that much of an ordeal on the first exercise. *These things must be the real deal.* 'How many of them am I testing?' she asked.

'Four.'

'That's not that many.'

'These things aren't cheap to make. We have four bots with working AIs who have been up and running for months and have already developed personalities with their own idiosyncrasies. All four have passed every test set before them with flying colours. They're ready.'

'And when you say "minimally staffed", what exactly are we looking at?'

'As I say, it's pretty minimal. You will be the only one in the field with them. I don't want too many prying eyes and I don't want instruction by committee. This is as real as it gets for this programme. The camp itself is just north of the Brecon Beacons and will be staffed by a small number of British military personnel. They're there to keep the camp running and to assist you in any way possible.'

'How will you know how it's going? Do I need to phone in and give you updates or just produce a report at the end?'

'We'll be able to track each bot's video feed, as well as track all telemetry. We'll know exactly what's going on with each one at all times. As for you, we'll kit you out with cameras and a few other bits and pieces, too.'

'Your own little reality show.'

'Indeed.'

Zaheera realised how much had been put into this programme. Her mother wasn't messing around. At the very least, she owed it to the woman who'd already lost one family member and very nearly another to give it her best shot. 'When do I start?' she asked.

'As soon as you get out of here.'

'I'm not sure Dr Griffiths has plans on letting me out any time soon.'

'I've already spoken to him. You're being released today.'

9

Zaheera unscrewed her empty thermos and filled it to the brim with black filtered coffee. No milk, no sugar. Just the drug, as her father would have said. The cookhouse at the Brecon Training Camp was a relatively basic affair: a few long tables with wooden benches and a top table for training staff. As her mother had promised, the entire training facility had been vacated by its usual inhabitants, and was now at her disposal. She'd been given a few British troops to keep the camp running and support her in any way she saw fit. The training operation was to be seen as a joint partnership between British and American forces with Cappelli Technologies providing the hardware of the future. Her second in command for the duration of the training was to be Captain Robertson, a short Scotsman with an even shorter fuse. At a full stretch, Captain Robertson just about reached Zaheera's chin. In her short stay at the Brecon Training Camp so far he'd walked around with a permanent scowl on his face, his red cheeks and pulsating forehead vein giving Zaheera the impression that at any point he was going to spontaneously combust.

Whenever he spoke, to her or his subordinates, he spoke in short, sharp bursts that brought to mind the image of a Scottish terrier barking at a postman. His moustache was not entirely dissimilar to a Scottish terrier's coat. Whether because of his nationality or because others had picked up on the resemblance, Zaheera had heard him referred to around the camp as Scottie.

'Right, we're all set, Major Bhukari,' Captain Robertson said as he approached Zaheera. 'They should be here any minute now.'

'Thank you, Captain,' she replied, and blew on her coffee as she looked out at the Welsh countryside from the cookhouse. The sky was a patchwork of grey clouds pouring with rain, as it had been from the moment she'd arrived a couple of days ago. The rain here was different to New York. It was soft but constant, like a never-ending torture technique designed to rob one of the will to live. The wet got right into the very core of your being, so that your soul itself was diluted to the point of insignificance. The ground, she knew from her walks around so far, was a soggy mess that would make traversing it a nightmare. Despite wanting to, Zaheera couldn't even be glad that the bots would be tested in these conditions. British weather was something Zaheera wouldn't wish on her worst enemy. Besides, she was going to have to be out there with them every step of the way. Afghanistan's dry heat and cool, starlit nights were actually an inviting prospect right now.

She pulled the hood of her olive poncho up and headed out into the rain. The wet ground squelched beneath her feet, giving up water like a sponge being squeezed. Captain Robertson muttered something under his breath about Edinburgh at least having a good view when it rained. Zaheera, quite enjoying how the pitter-patter of rain drowned out most of what he grumbled about, chose not to engage him in conversation. Instead she stood at ease, face forward, sipping at her morning addiction.

A large black van with blacked-out windows made its way onto the premises, along with another two vehicles behind it, and came to a stop in front of Zaheera and Captain Roberston. Zaheera nodded to her mother in the passenger seat of the van, who got out and slid open the side door. Out stepped the bot that had robbed Zaheera of her dignity in their short scuffle not so long ago. She recalled it being named Alpha. Alpha got out of the van and stood to attention a few paces in front of her, followed shortly after by three other almost identical humanoid robots.

Each bot stood roughly two metres tall, with the same dark hard-shell armour encasing its wired musculature. They all had the same identical white LED lights for eyes and speakers for mouths. In what Zaheera had guessed was a move by her mother to help with identification, each bot had a name on their chest. Their names were Alpha, Bravo, Charlie and Delta. *Real creative, Mom.* In addition to this, each bot's skull was very slightly tinted a different colour for identification. Alpha's was black all over, Bravo's was navy blue, Charlie's yellow and Delta's red.

Zaheera paced around the bots once, eyeing them up and down, looking for defects. She found none. She circled back to her original position in front of them. 'Welcome to Brecon Training Camp. I'm Major Bhukari. You may call me Major Bhukari. This here,' she gestured towards the captain, 'is Captain Robertson. Consider us your guardians for the foreseeable future. That means it's up to us what you do and when you do it. Now, I'm not one of those loud-and-proud instructors, so if I don't like what I see, I'm just going to fail you and send you back so they can strip you for parts. There won't be any song and dance from me. Got it?'

The bots all nodded.

'Got it?' she asked again.

'Yes, Major,' they answered in unison.

They learn fast. 'Good. Now apparently you lot have designs on being grunts. Or at least you were designed to be grunts. I'm not about to just suggest to my higher-ups that they replace the world's finest soldiers with a bunch of over-sized toys, so you better not waste my time.'

'Right, you mechanical bastards,' Captain Roberson shouted. 'Follow me.'

The bots followed him in single-file formation to get acquainted with the various locations within the camp.

Zaheera walked over to her mother. 'All set?'

'Yep. My lot will be out of your way the whole time.' She pointed towards the individuals unpacking various cases of computer equipment and carrying them into a nearby building, which had been kept free for them. 'They'll do all their monitoring through the equipment. You won't even notice them being here.'

'And where will you be?'

'I'm heading back to HQ,' her mother said. 'Nobody wants their mother around to watch over them whilst they work, I know that. I'll be checking in with my team multiple times a day, but I'm leaving this in your capable hands. You know how to get a hold of me if you need to.' She squeezed Zaheera's shoulder tightly with one hand. 'Good luck.'

ZAHEERA MADE her way down to the obstacle course where Captain Robertson was yelling a plethora of indecipherable expletives at the bots who, to their credit, looked completely unfazed by the verbal abuse. *Either that, or they haven't got a clue what he's saying.*

She took her place next to him and waited for him to finish his cursing. 'Thank you, Captain. Now, let's not all stand on ceremony. Corporal,' she said to the baby-faced lad eyeballing the bots like his childhood toys had come to life, 'care to show this lot how it's done?'

'Yes, Major,' the boy replied.

'Off you go, then.'

The corporal set off at a blistering speed around the obstacle course, which started with the brick wall. He got both arms up and then levered his legs to the right as he went up and over with the grace of a gymnast. A pretty sodden gymnast, but a gymnast nonetheless. Zaheera was glad she'd picked him. He might actually set a tough time. He ran up to the steel-framed rope walk and moved swiftly across, before sliding down the pole and running through a minefield of old tyres, up over the raised wooden beams and into the river where soldiers were positioned either side of a tight-fitting tunnel. He dived into the water without a moment's hesitation and popped out the other side of the tunnel a second later to rapturous applause, whereby he got to his feet, made it out of the water and did a beeline back to the start.

'Not bad, Corporal. Not bad at all.'

The youngster, panting heavily but attempting not to show it, nodded and made his way back to his original position.

'You,' Zaheera said, pointing at Alpha, who was currently tapping some water out of the side of its tilted head, 'stop messing with your booger hook and get after it.'

'Yes, Major.'

She knew it before it started. Hell, she knew it the

minute the bastard had put her on the ground multiple times in succession back at her mother's office in London. Why she'd hoped for a different result she didn't know, but seeing the bot take off faster than the corporal pissed her off more than she expected. Her blood boiled. She squeezed her fists in frustration as it stomped around the course in half the corporal's time before standing to attention in its original position as if nothing had happened.

'No medals for noise, Metalzilla. I'm pretty sure they heard your heavy ass stomping around back in London. Speed means nothing if the enemy can hear you a mile off, you bag of spare parts. Again.' She pointed at the wall and watched as the bot set off again.

All day she made the four bots run the course, offering no praise for the constantly improved times nor for their dramatically improved stealth. She chose not to voice her surprise at the speed at which their learning appeared to set in. None of them ever needed to be given an instruction twice. All day they trudged through the mud and the rain until the assault course looked more like a bog than a training facility. Her mother had informed her that they could go days without needing to recharge or replace batteries and offload non-essential data from their hard drives, so there was no hope in running them into the ground in one day. As the sun set, despite a lack of evidence of its original existence from behind the rain-filled clouds, Zaheera eventually relented and ordered everybody back to their quarters to clean up and get some shut-eye ahead of the next day's weapons test and march.

ZAHEERA ROSE AT DAWN, grateful that the rain had stopped at some point during the night. She knew that hoping for a sunny day was too much, but she was glad that she might be able to at least stay dry for a few hours if this day went to plan.

She hopped out of bed and got into her fatigues without turning the light on. Privacy in the military had always been in short supply and despite having a room to herself on this occasion, old habits died hard. Grabbing her trusty thermos from her bedside locker, she made her way down to the bots' quarters. Each bot was standing at the end of its bed in some kind of standby mode. The nearest bot, Delta, turned his red head towards her as the LED light serving as a visual representation of his eyes turned on. Its mechanical brethren did likewise.

'Good morning, Major,' they said in unison.

Zaheera realised for the first time that each bot's voice was male. She hadn't thought much of it the day before, but now wondered whether this was an intentional decision of her mother's which might reflect on her opinion of Zaheera's career choice. She decided not to pursue that particular disaster zone and ordered the bots to be ready outside in ten, knowing, of course, that they were ready to go at a moment's notice. On her way out she passed the cookhouse and grabbed a quick bite to eat with Captain Robertson, who was looking miserable as ever. He accompanied her outside and marched the bots down to the firing range.

The firing range consisted of an enclosed area set up with targets from which soldiers could either fire from a set position towards the back, or walk through a small shooting assault course. Surrounding the firing range was a mock village, intended for more dynamic drills.

She started them out with pistols and assault rifles, measuring their speed, accuracy, and ability to avoid civilian targets. Each bot handled its weapon as if it were an extension of its own form, gently releasing the trigger and firing as accurately as Zaheera believed was possible with each weapon. She had figured this would be the case; if there was one area where she had expected a certain level of prowess, it was with a weapon. They all had advanced AI and measurement tools unavailable in a human to measure precise wind speeds, elevation, lighting. There was no guesswork here. Each bot was able to avoid every civilian target, too, which ruined her chances of criticising their ability to judge.

'You ever seen shooting like this before?' Captain Robertson asked.

She didn't answer.

LATER THAT EVENING, after the afternoon's march, in which each bot had again excelled, Zaheera returned her metal candidates to the Cappelli Technologies team based in the free house so that they could be recharged, checked for errors, and hard drives purged of unnecessary data ahead of the field test.

The engineer, a young woman named Susie, asked Zaheera how the training had gone so far.

'Weren't you watching on video?'

'I was, but they didn't always catch your sourpuss reactions.'

'Sounds like you saw enough, then.'

'You know,' Susie said, 'we're not just out here trying to rob your jobs or whatever it is you think we're trying to do that's got you so pissed off. We believe in them.'

'Yeah, well, I believed in my old pickup truck, but that piece of shit died on me on my way to the store one day. Just upped and quit, right there in the middle of the road. I had to put a call out to have someone tow me and that hump of steel back to the station. What if that happens to these things in battle, huh? You think we can just call a timeout so we can send little old Susie out to recharge 'em? You think our enemies have time for that shit?'

'I'd rather we were sending someone out to battle zones with spare batteries than empty coffins.'

Zaheera grabbed Susie by the collar and shoved her against the wall. 'Why don't you save your idealism for your blog post, huh? Leave the fighting to those of us who signed up for it.'

'Both my brothers signed up for it,' Susie said. 'You know what that got them? A one-way ticket home in a cheap pine box. So why don't you save your anger for the bottle? Leave the fixing to those of us who signed up for it.'

'Is something wrong?' one of the bots asked.

Zaheera turned to see Bravo standing behind her. 'Who asked you to step out of formation?'

'Apologies, Major. We were concerned for Miss Edwards' safety. My analysis—'

'"*We* were concerned"? In what line of code does it say you can plot together to decide when a human interaction is deemed acceptable or not?'

The bot faltered.

'I thought so. Now get the fuck back into line before I have Susie here dismantle you and lock you in storage for the foreseeable future.'

'Yes, Major. My apologies.'

Bravo stepped out of the room into the hallway to rejoin its brethren.

'You know, you shouldn't speak to them like that,' Susie

said. 'Everything they witness is a new learning. We should really be showing them the best of humanity.'

'Why the fuck are you designing them for war, then?'

'Because that's where governments spend most of their money. Maybe one day we'll branch out. Maybe one day we can have bots that work in factories and hospitals, too. Maybe one day we can liberate our own species from dangerous jobs altogether. Imagine a world where we can be free to follow our dreams, to *truly* follow our dreams. Will you still hate these bots then?'

'Will I still be stuck listening to your gospel?'

ZAHEERA'S MOTHER called her as she was getting into bed and asked how everything was going so far.

'Well, Susie and I are becoming fast friends.'

'Be nice, she has a good heart.'

'It's not the heart I have an issue with. It's the self-righteous opinions coming out of her trap every few seconds that I'm finding rather infuriating.'

'Let Susie worry about Susie. How are my bots doing?'

Zaheera placed her phone down and climbed into bed. 'Mom?'

'Yes, dear.'

'You remember when Dad used to say that you should always trust your gut, no matter what?'

'I do.'

'Well, I don't like them. We're not meant to have machines replacing us, no matter what function they serve.'

Her mother tutted on the screen. 'Oh, give it a rest, Zaheera. Technology has always been used to improve our way of life. From the days of Stone Age tools like hammerstones and sharp stone flakes, we've constantly evolved as a species to improve our way of life. This is just the next logical step. Do you really think your soldier friend with the wife and kid—'

'Rodriguez.'

'Yes, Rodriguez. Do you really think he wouldn't gladly have given up his career to spend more time with his wife and kid?'

Zaheera fought the urge to argue back. In truth she wasn't sure. Rodriguez had been a fine soldier and she couldn't imagine a bot doing a better job of it. But would he have given up the only career he knew to watch his little girl grow up? Perhaps. In fact, he'd been planning on leaving, if what his wife had told her was true. What was it about soldiers that had them planning their post-military lives from the moment they joined? She had never thought of being anything other than a soldier.

Her mother, apparently sensing her troubled mind, stepped in. 'Look, Zaheera. I can't force you to like these things, but they are here. They exist. So maybe rather than giving them a hard time all through training – yes, I've seen the videos – maybe you should actually train them, like you would a normal soldier, and see what potential you can unlock. You might just surprise yourself, and if you let them, they might surprise you.'

10

Zaheera and the four bots left at dawn the next day. Susie had informed Zaheera that they were all fully charged and could last anywhere between three days and a week before their next charge, depending on how much they exerted themselves in that time. Similarly, their hard drives would start to fill after a number of days and if not returned to her for review, they would start to self-select which data to delete and which to keep. All of which meant that Zaheera could keep them out for a few days without much concern. The exercise she'd planned with Captain Robertson wasn't exactly like SERE training because of the bots' limited battery life, so the first few days was intended as an introduction to survival and evasion techniques. It meant long hours and sleeping rough, just what Zaheera liked, and it would be a good way of clearing her mind of flashbacks from Afghanistan, which had haunted her every sleep since. She hoped this would at least wear her out to such a point that her brain might finally give her a rest. Being in the field was always where she was most at ease.

They covered a lot of ground the first day; Zaheera wanted to see how they managed rough terrain. Not bad, it turned out. They hiked over Pen y Fan, a picturesque mountain which provided views of the surrounding area, crossing numerous fields and streams along the way.

'How far are we going?' Charlie asked as afternoon turned to twilight.

'Not much further,' Zaheera replied. 'We need to make camp before nightfall. Any sign of a tail, Delta?'

'Negative,' the bot pulling up the rear said. Zaheera had tasked it with keeping an eye out for Captain Roberts and his team who would be out against them.

They came over a dip on the edge of a wood where they were sheltered on two sides by the wood and the hill.

'Here,' Zaheera said. 'This is where we're going to make camp. Bravo, do a quick recce of the wood and make sure we haven't got any surprises waiting for us in there. Delta, do a scan of the other side of the hill. Any problems, we move on to another spot. Alpha and Charlie, you two help me set up a bivvy.'

'Yes, Major,' the bots all replied in unison.

As Bravo and Delta headed off on their recces, Zaheera led Alpha and Charlie in the collecting of sticks, branches and stones to help build a shelter. By the time they had collected what she deemed enough, the other two had returned with confirmation that the spot was clear of enemies.

Zaheera showed the bots how to set up a makeshift bivouac shelter using the logs as frames and the smaller sticks and stones to round out the rest of the structure. Once complete she instructed them to cover it in leaves and ferns. Finally, they placed their bivouac sheets on the ground as groundsheets to give them some separation from the soaked earth beneath.

With camp complete, she set about clearing a space in front of the shelter and put the remaining stones in a circle to serve as the perimeter for the fireplace. The bots watched with keen interest, assisting at her instruction.

'Why are we making a fire?' Alpha asked.

'What do you mean "Why are we making a fire"? It's part of your training. I need to see that you're capable of performing basic survival skills.'

'But *we* wouldn't need a fire,' Alpha replied. 'We're not dependent on maintaining a certain temperature. We also don't need the shelter you just made us put up to protect us from the elements. These seem like tasks based on human frailties.'

Zaheera eyed the bot suspiciously. She couldn't tell if it was making a slight or asking a genuine question out of curiosity. It was impossible to understand tone and context with these machines. *Are they even capable of contempt?* She didn't know. These were not questions she had thought to ask her mother. In her mind, they were just tools awaiting instruction. Despite her mother's information about their ability to learn and think for themselves, she hadn't thought of this in the context of forming opinions.

'Look,' she said, 'the way I see it, there isn't a single military force in the world that has enough government funding to replace its entire troop headcount with you lot, so I'm thinking that whatever your involvement, it'll be a slow integration. Which means, my little mechanical halfwit, that if you do end up in the military instead of stacking shelves down at the local grocery store, you'll have to work with fellow soldiers. Real soldiers. And you know what real soldiers do?' She didn't wait for a response. 'They look out for one another. Just in the same way you might need someone to give you a charge once in a while or help download data from your drives while you're out in the field, you'll need to protect the men and women you serve with. That means you'll need to learn how to set up camp, how to build a fire, how to cook and clean and do first aid. You want to be a real grunt, you gotta earn that privilege.'

Alpha took a moment to mull this over. The bot sat still, as if locked deep in thought, trying to assess the information it had just been given and arrive at a logical conclusion.

'It seems to me,' Alpha said after a minor eternity, 'that it would make more sense for humans to just get out of the way and leave it to those who can do the work better.'

'What did you say?'

'I mean simply that these menial tasks need only be learned if we're going to have to cohabit with humans, but if we were given true autonomy, we'd quite easily function on our own. It would be far more efficient. Humans could simply step out of the way. The way I see it, the choice is yours.'

'Alpha,' Charlie cut in, 'remember your place.' The bot turned to Zaheera, who was staring into the now lit fire, and implored, 'Alpha does not speak for all of us, Major Bhukari.'

Bravo and Delta nodded in agreement as they joined the circle around the fire.

'That's quite all right, Charlie, thank you. I'm sure Alpha's questions were out of genuine curiosity.'

'Of course,' Alpha said. 'I'll go get us more wood.'

The bot trotted into the trees as the sun lost its battle with the horizon and the evening succumbed to darkness. Zaheera stared into the flames and mulled over Alpha's comments. Its logic, taken from its own perspective, was sound enough, but that didn't make it at all comforting. The other three hadn't shown any sign of similar thought process. Suddenly the weight of her assessment at the end of the four-week course dawned on her. This was more than just a test drive of some machinery. These were sentient beings and she needed to be keeping an eye out for more than just their shooting abilities.

After she'd eaten – the bots having checked themselves over and cleaned what parts required cleaning – Zaheera instructed Bravo to keep first watch while the others went into standby mode to conserve their energy for the next day. She tucked herself in under the makeshift shelter. For the first time since leaving Afghanistan, she felt comfortable again. The surroundings suited her well. She liked the slight discomfort of camping, the smell of smoke as the fire died down so that only the glowing embers provided any light. She thought of Rodriguez and Johnson, and what she'd give to be out on exercise with them right now, maybe playing a little I-Spy or some other shit time-filling game. Johnson would likely have had plenty to say about camping out in the cold and wet Welsh hills with a bunch of machines for company.

Her muscles ached from the day's hiking. It was a good ache. The kind of ache where your body lets you know it's still got a little something to give. Recalling happier times with her team sitting around fires in much warmer climates, Zaheera slipped into a deep sleep.

Delta shook Zaheera awake with a violence she figured it was incapable of comprehending. 'All right, I'm up. No need to dislodge my shoulder in the process.' She blinked away her slumber and surveyed her surroundings. The mountainside was covered in a morning fog so thick she couldn't see much beyond the fire pit, which Bravo was attending to. 'What's up?' she asked.

'It's the others, we can't find them.'

'Who?'

'Alpha and Charlie.'

'What do you mean you can't find them?'

'I mean they seem to have disappeared.'

Zaheera sat bolt upright. 'When was the last time you saw them?'

'I took over Bravo's watch just after midnight. Charlie took over my watch a couple of hours later. That was the last time I saw them. When I awoke this morning, both Charlie and Alpha were gone. Bravo hasn't seen them either.'

'Okay, let's scan the immediate area. Any sign of Captain Robertson and his squad overnight?'

'Negative, no sign of anybody else in the immediate vicinity.'

They dug a hole in the ground and buried the last remnants of the fire before covering the hole up and taking the shelter down. By the time they were done only a trained eye would have known that anybody had spent the night there. Some of the morning fog had lifted and the trio set off in a line, spaced twenty feet apart, to look for signs of their two missing team members. Zaheera asked both bots to use their internal scanning systems to check for signs of movement in the area, but both came up short. She thought back to her planning meeting with Captain Robertson just in case she'd missed something, but knew she was being ridiculous even doubting herself. She and Scottie had not discussed any overnight camp raids and there certainly hadn't been any discussion whatsoever about the taking of prisoners. Whatever was going on wasn't happening according to their plan. She wondered if one of the bots had fallen down a ravine or been swept away in river current. There were plenty of small streams in the area, but she doubted there was anything powerful enough to drag one of these things away. *Maybe they just malfunctioned. Some buggy glitch that's set them off and now they're sitting in the grass somewhere completely oblivious to the rest of us trying to figure out where they are.* 'Bravo.'

'Yes, Major?'

'Have you tried communicating with each other, you know, by non-verbal means? Have you tried beaming a signal out to see if you get a response?'

'Yes, Major. Nothing so far in response.'

Shit.

Having had no luck checking the mountainside, they moved into the wood and scanned through the trees. Zaheera was reminded of the hunting trips she'd taken with her dad as a kid. They'd head out of New York for the weekend and hook up with her father's friends. Together they'd all head to the Adirondack mountain region, where they could escape off the beaten path and spend some time hunting deer. Zaheera wasn't allowed a gun until well into her teens, but she'd joined the expeditions as a young kid, learning how the hunt was carried out. She learned how to walk quietly through the woods without stepping on anything that might crunch or come loose, she learned how to slow her breathing and how not to talk for hours on end, operating entirely on hand signals. When she was eventually trained how to fire a weapon she quickly became one of the most valuable assets to the team, often taking the record for longest or most difficult shot.

Now she called on all her experience to look for the two missing bots. It was all about noticing the unusual: a broken twig, a scrape in the ground, a dropped utensil or item of clothing, not that it would be an item of clothing on this occasion. Not unless somebody else was involved, which she told herself she shouldn't rule out at this stage.

The wood provided no luck. It was completely untouched, save for the initial extremity they had passed at the start where Zaheera knew Alpha had walked around collecting dry sticks and twigs.

'Shall we call it in?' Delta asked as they came out the other side of the wood.

Zaheera looked around. She couldn't see anything obvious in the valley below. It was deadly quiet, too. Just a slight rustle of branches as the wind blew through the trees to her back. 'Not yet,' she said. 'We'll make our way down to the bottom and if nothing's there, then we'll call it in.'

Halfway down to the bottom Zaheera noticed a depression in the earth that looked like it was machine-made. The wet earth had given way under something of considerable weight. The surrounding grass, too, was flatter near the depression than the rest of the area. Morning dew coated the whole scene, confirming to Zaheera that whatever had happened here had happened the night before. She called Bravo and Delta over for their analysis. Both confirmed that it looked very much like something similar to them had passed through this area and by Bravo's estimation had potentially fallen over here.

They fanned out again, on full alert. The assault rifles they were carrying contained blank rounds and would be of no help whatsoever if anything actually went down. On Zaheera's instruction, the bots stowed their guns and unsheathed the knives they had all been given.

A set of bot's tracks led all the way down to a small river winding its way around the valley floor. The tracks confused Zaheera. Each depression was light and well-placed, as if the bot making them had been walking at a slow, casual pace. Had it been running from something, or after something, the depressions would have broken the earth up. The spacing between each depression would also likely have been farther apart. No, whatever the reason behind this bot's movement, it had moved slowly and cautiously through the night.

The tracks came to a stop at the river. Zaheera scanned the water as it rushed between rocks and slipped around the bend. No sign of anything on the riverbed. The morning sun appeared over the top of the mountain above and warmed her face as the fog dissipated. She found no tracks coming out of the other side of the river opposite where the tracks went in. 'The tracks come in here but don't come out the other side,' she said to the bots. 'That means that whichever bot it was, it probably moved through the river before coming out somewhere else. Bravo, you take the left. Delta, you take the right. I'm going to check the land directly ahead, just in case I was wrong about nothing coming out of the water here. If either of you see anything, you holler, all right?'

'Yes, Major,' they both replied.

Zaheera climbed out onto the riverbank on the far side and started looking for tracks. *Why the hell would a bot feel the need to move through a river to cover its tracks?* Something wasn't right about the situation. She racked her brain for an answer but came up short. Nobody outside of a few US and UK military personnel and key members of Cappelli Technologies even knew about the field test. She knew that a number of government officials were in the loop as regards funding and signing off the programme, but in terms of anybody knowing about this specific test, her mother had tried to keep the number involved to an absolute minimum.

No other rival technology companies were aware, nor any other militaries. Prior to the disappearance of Alpha and Charlie, Zaheera had assumed the person most keen for this programme to fail was herself.

'Major?'

Zaheera couldn't tell which bot had called out for her.

'Major, you might want to come take a look at this.'

Delta. 'On my way, Delta.' She hopped over to the bot's location just beyond the bend in the river. Delta was standing still in the water, pointing at something on the far bank. Zaheera's eyes followed the bot's fingers until she saw it. On the edge of the bank, water still running over it, threatening to pull it downstream, was the yellow-tinged skull of Charlie. Problem was, the bot seemed to be missing the rest of its body.

She leapt into the water and strode over to the dismembered skull. It showed no sign of life. Its lights were out and the LED screen had been smashed in by some kind of blunt force trauma. The whole skull had taken some kind of beating. Zaheera knelt in the water and picked it up, turning it over in her hands. The back of the skull lay open and ripped wires dangled out. A number of parts from within the skull appeared to be missing as various open slots became visible in the light.

'Is everything all right, Major?' Delta asked.

'No. No, everything is not all right. Go get Bravo and help me look for Charlie's body. There might be more clues around here.'

It wasn't long before they found Charlie's body not far from where its head had been lying. The body was caught in some rocks, which had halted its river cruise. Upon closer inspection, Zaheera saw that Charlie's body had also sustained some fairly serious trauma. Whatever had happened, Charlie hadn't been a willing participant.

'It's very strange,' Bravo said when Zaheera asked what could have inflicted such damage on Charlie. 'Our armour is designed to survive everything from small-arms fire to major impacts. Whoever or whatever did this to Charlie knew exactly where to hit and how hard to hit. The state of Charlie's skull is perhaps more concerning, though.'

'Why is that?'

'Because several key components have been removed, including hard drives, CPU and batteries.'

'What does that mean?'

'It means that Charlie's attacker didn't attack out of self-defence. Also Charlie wasn't just some random target – the missing components prove that. Charlie was very much the intended target.'

Zaheera's fears were confirmed. She pulled out her radio and attempted to contact the Brecon Training Camp but the radio just gave off a dead static. 'Fuck. Delta, call it in.'

Delta tapped a button on its skull and spoke. 'Brecon One, this is Greenhorn, over.'

Nothing.

'I repeat, Brecon One, this is Greenhorn. Do you read? Over.'

Nothing.

The bot turned the volume up of the signal it was receiving. Static crackled through the air that sent a shiver down Zaheera's spine.

Bravo turned to Zaheera, who was now doing everything in her power not to show her trembling body. 'Major, I think we're being hunted.'

11

'What do you mean, you think we're being hunted?' Zaheera asked Bravo.

'It seems illogical to me that someone should try to destroy one of us without having some reason,' the bot replied. 'Our design uses some of the toughest materials currently available, whilst allowing for us to maintain our speed and agility. We know that whatever attacked Charlie was aware of what to go for. Now, with all radio signals failing, I am confident that this was a considered move.'

'Have you tried changing your frequency?' Zaheera asked, doing the same on her own radio.

'Affirmative. No luck. There's something else, too.'

'What?'

'I cannot connect to the cloud.'

'My connection to the cloud has also been severed,' Delta added.

Zaheera racked her brain for a logical reason. 'We're in a valley, no?'

'Yes,' Bravo replied.

'Well, it might just be a signalling issue. We need to get to higher ground and see if we can perhaps get a proper signal from there. It seems strange to me that all of our comms went down the moment we dropped into this valley.'

'That *may* be a possibility.'

Finally, emotion. Zaheera figured the bots were learning the subtle nuances of intonation based on their experiences with her. It helped her confidence in understanding what Bravo was trying to convey. 'Well, while it's still a possibility, I'm not going to rule it out. Now, let's see what we can salvage from Charlie. There may still be something of use that points us in the right direction. I assume your hard drives are not stored only in your skulls?'

'That is correct,' Delta said. 'We have backup drives stored behind our chest plates. The lead plates are perhaps the strongest part of our structure, or at least the part best designed to withstand small-arms fire. I will check for you,' the ever-helpful bot said.

Zaheera was amazed by the various idiosyncratic personalities each bot had and how recognisable they were becoming. Delta's main prerogative appeared to be one of constant assistance. It never wanted to let her down. Bravo was more decisive, questioning what didn't make sense, much like Alpha had done the night before. Charlie had defended Zaheera by criticising Alpha when it had questioned her about whether bots should be made to learn such menial tasks as building fires and shelters. They each had some unique quality; she wondered whether these had been pre-installed or were something that developed organically. She doubted the bots were aware either way so it wasn't worth asking.

The two bots carried Charlie's body out of the river and placed it down in the grass not far from the bank. Zaheera followed, still carrying Charlie's dented skull, which she set down near the body so the bots could work on it undisturbed. She felt a strange sense of loss, tinged with guilt, like she had often felt when one of her team had been worked on by a medic in the heat of battle. Usually in that situation there was screaming and bullets flying, kicking up dirt around them. These tranquil surroundings made Zaheera more uncomfortable. It was unnatural to her.

With Bravo's assistance, Delta set about taking Charlie apart. The bot worked with an efficiency and precision that impressed Zaheera. She looked down at her shaking hand and realised she was glad the bot was running the operation. The idea occurred to her that a bot performing a surgery could be far more accurate than a human. Perhaps her mother had been right in seeing the potential of these things. Finesse had been a strength of each one throughout their training so far. Each had excelled in all manner of physical activities, with pinpoint accuracy when it came to shooting. She wondered just how deadly a team of these bots could be on the battlefield. All without the need to have little girls left at home wondering why their fathers were never coming home.

Delta opened Charlie's chest cavity and dug around inside. 'That's odd,' it said.

'What's odd?' Zaheera asked. 'The hard drives are there, right?'

'They're there, but they've been damaged. By what, I do not know. My best guess is some kind of electric shock.'

'How the hell is that possible?'

'I'm not quite sure. Our design allows us to move through water without any risk to ourselves. However, if parts of our armour were opened up, it is possible that we would then be susceptible to a kind of electric shock. Charlie's presence in the river is likely to have exacerbated whatever shock was inflicted.'

Zaheera felt around on her belt at the mention of this. A moment later she had her answer. Her eyes widened as the realisation dawned on her.

'What is it?' Bravo asked.

'My belt. The was an EMP grenade on it. Nothing too powerful, just enough to give one of you a fright if I felt you weren't taking me seriously enough. But it would have been a lot more effective if the target were in the water when the grenade went off, especially if the target's armour had been tampered with.'

'That means the attacker was able to remove the grenade from your belt before attacking Charlie.'

'Yes, yes it does,' Zaheera said.

'Alpha,' Bravo said.

'I'm afraid so,' she said. 'We need to get to higher ground now.'

They moved as fast as they could, leaving Charlie's remains beside the riverbed, and made it back to the top of the mountain in half the time it had taken them to make it down. Zaheera tried to use her own radio first but was met with the same infuriating static she had experienced by the river. 'You try,' she said to Bravo.

'Nothing, I'm afraid,' the bot said a moment later. 'Just static.'

'Fuck,' she said, before berating herself for letting her subordinates witness her lapse in self-control. 'Bravo, scan the immediate vicinity and see what you pick up.'

'I can't,' the bot replied. 'I need to connect to the cloud to use services beyond my basic functions. Right now I'm running in a standard offline mode. Delta, too.'

The other bot confirmed Bravo's point with a nod of the head.

'So you're telling me Alpha has somehow managed to successfully attack and kill one of you and take the rest of you offline?'

'Affirmative,' Bravo replied.

'Well that's just fucking fantastic, isn't it? Surely you have some kind of code in your make-up which prevents you from becoming some kind of rogue killing machine?'

'I do,' Bravo said, 'as does Delta, and Charlie, before … well, *before*.'

'And Alpha?'

'Alpha is unique.'

'I swear to whatever artificial god you serve, I'm going to make what happened to Charlie look like a fucking scratch if you don't start being a bit more forthcoming with your information, machine,' Zaheera said, giving up all pretence of self-control.

'Alpha is not like us,' Delta said, desirous, as ever, to be of assistance. 'We were all made after Alpha. Each of us was installed with various security functions which prevent us from acting in certain ways, despite whatever evidence is placed in front of us. Our characteristics were designed to be quite Asimovian in theory. We're intended to be obedient, helpful, and never a threat to human life until instructed otherwise.'

'Really helps me feel safe when you're holding an assault rifle. So, what, Alpha can do whatever the fuck it wants?'

'In short, yes. Alpha has some basic code to ensure safety, but was designed to develop free will.'

'How can you be sure of that?'

'We can read most of each other's code when we

communicate with one another. Alpha's code is missing a lot of what ours contains.'

Zaheera thought back to her first meeting with Alpha and how the bot appeared to have had some kind of bond with her mother. She had kept it in the open, smack in the middle of her office floor, not chained up or locked away. The bot had even asked if Ameera considered it a friend and she had said yes. *It wanted to be her friend, for fuck's sake.* What kind of crazy did you have to be to design a machine to be neurotic and insecure? Perhaps that developed naturally as the AI developed, she figured. *Maybe we're all that neurotic by design.*

What she couldn't understand was why her mother would design such a thing in the first place? Its purpose wasn't immediately apparent. Her mother had gone on about the potential of these things to create a safer world, but giving one of them free will? Wasn't that just opening the door to disaster? Whatever her mother's cavalier reasoning, Zaheera was now stuck facing a rogue AI hell-bent on destroying its competition. She wondered whether she would be considered as being in Alpha's way. 'Why would Alpha have it in for you?' she asked. 'Or was it just Charlie?'

'Inconclusive,' Bravo replied.

'Is it because Charlie stood up for me when Alpha was questioning my teaching methods? Would that have caused such significant offence as to warrant an attack?'

'Offence is perhaps a stretch,' Delta said. 'Although, given Alpha's unique make-up, it may be possible. We are not, in theory, designed to have emotional reactions. Anything you perceive as emotional is likely our artificial intelligence learning a pattern of speech considered similar to your own.'

'But something has caused Alpha to go rogue. Whatever

the cause, perhaps before this training, it was certainly confirmed by being on this training. Which means something you or I have done or said has caused Alpha to react this way.'

'That is possible,' Bravo said. 'It may also be possible that someone has taken control of Alpha. We are routinely controlled by various Cappelli Technologies personnel whilst on company premises.'

'So it's possible Alpha is not acting of its own volition?'

'Correct.'

Fuck me.

'What do we do now?' Delta asked.

'First, we head for camp. Alpha may well still be after us, so let's keep eyes and ears – figuratively for you two, of course – open. If we make it back to camp, we may find a way out of this.'

ZAHEERA KNEW that making it back to camp by the end of the day was far too ambitious. Their first day's hike away from camp had been a long and arduous one that had begun early in the morning. They had already lost most of the current morning looking for Charlie and then subsequently analysing Charlie's remains, all but guaranteeing that they would need to camp at least one night on the way back to Brecon Training Camp. All local roads had been closed to the public for the exercise, making their chances of flagging down a civilian vehicle impossible. Their best hope was to make a straight shot for camp to see whether Alpha had passed that way. From there they would be able to analyse the situation and react accordingly. Zaheera hoped everybody back at camp was okay. Alpha might not have been carrying any live ammunition but the bot had already proved just how dangerous it could be.

A headache ripped savagely through her head as her mind went into overdrive considering all the different ways Alpha might find them while they were out in the open. Both Bravo and Delta could likely make it back to camp in one go by hiking through the night, but she knew she didn't have it in her – not without severely affecting her capabilities. No, she needed to stay sharp. And to be rested was to be sharp. She took her water bottle off her belt and poured some of the contents into her hand, splashing her face and the back of her neck. The cool water was a welcome relief on her sweat-drenched skin. She inspected her hair, which was filled with small leaves and twigs, but she was in no mood for personal hygiene. Water, food and a safe place to sleep were her only concerns before sundown. That and the homicidal robot terrorising the Welsh countryside, of course.

Zaheera considered Bravo's point about Alpha potentially being controlled by somebody else from a remote location. She didn't voice her concern but she deliberated internally over the possibility of Bravo and Delta having the same thing happen to them and what this might mean for her own safety. Connected devices had been hacked since their very inception and Zaheera's confidence in security systems, especially given current circumstances, was somewhere between nil and sweet fuck all. She eyed both bots as they hiked over the crest of a hill, both just ahead of her in a single-file line. Their actions hadn't been erratic at all. Both had remained calm under pressure, with neither of them showing any cause for concern so far. She made a mental note to keep a close eye on it. It was suddenly apparent just how alone she was out in these hills. Taking on one of these bots in hand-to-hand combat would be nigh on impossible, let alone three, if her two current companions also turned on her.

She knew that she carried enough food on her for a couple more days out in the wilderness if it came to it, but that didn't make the prospect of staying out here much longer any more enticing. Her desire to get back to camp drove her onwards. Her muscles cried out for rest with every step but she ignored her body's protests. Now was not the time to start giving in to weakness.

'Keep your eyes peeled,' she reminded the bots. 'We might still run into Captain Robertson and his team. They're out here somewhere and probably completely unaware of Alpha's current situation.'

'Yes, Major,' both replied.

Zaheera wondered where the pint-sized captain and his squad had got to. She had neither seen nor heard a single trace of them since the exercise had begun. That was of course their original intention, but she hoped that, wherever they were, they were safe. Perhaps they'd even seen Alpha roaming the hillsides on its own and called it in. Probably just a pipe dream, though.

'Bravo?' she asked, a new thought running through her mind.

'Yes, Major?'

'If your connection to the cloud has been severed, wouldn't that have caused an alert to trigger in the software monitoring you? Shouldn't the people keeping an eye on that data have noticed that you've all suddenly gone offline?'

The bot thought on it for a second before confirming that this should in fact be true.

Hope.

It might be that young Susie back at camp had noticed

when all the bots had been taken offline. If so, she would hopefully have sent some of her team out to scout for the missing bots based on their last known locations or, even better in Zaheera's mind, had called it in to Cappelli Technologies back in London. Her mother would know what to do. If she'd been informed, this whole thing could be over in a matter of hours. *Come on, Susie. Do the right thing.* She hoped Susie wasn't the kind to fall asleep on the job. It didn't seem likely, but then, you never really knew how useless somebody was until they were thrown in at the deep end. The cowardly Sergeant Miller had probably passed all his tests with flying colours, but once he was stuck in that convoy back in Afghanistan, with bullets painting the windows of his vehicle red with the blood of his squad, he'd shut down, becoming completely ineffective and an eventual burden on the convoy survivors at the time. What a complete waste he'd been.

The group descended into a valley between two fairly small hills. At the bottom a small stream wound its way across the valley floor, leading into a thicket of trees. Zaheera needed to replenish her water supply. The thicket would at least provide some small semblance of cover. She instructed Bravo and Delta to head down and post out on either side of the stream.

The ice-cold water was clear as day, and after a few hours hiking, Zaheera needed its cool touch on her skin. She dropped her rucksack at the stream's edge and knelt over the water, drinking from it like a pig from a trough, dignity be damned.

Bravo and Delta patrolled in short circles on either side of the bank as Zaheera drenched her head underwater.

Zaheera was mid-sip when something dark burst from the nearby thicket at a pace Zaheera didn't think possible for any land animal. It took an eternal second for her to realise, with a dawning horror, that the man-shaped thing tearing towards her was Alpha.

'Run!' Bravo shouted; it was currently positioned on the same side of the stream as the one on which Alpha was running towards them.

In a heartbeat, Delta had Zaheera's rucksack slung over its back and grabbed her by the wrist. 'We need to move, *now*.'

Zaheera knew it wasn't messing about. She got to her feet and let the bot pull her from the river, almost taking her arm out of its socket as it did so. In no time at all they were at full sprint, headed for the crest of the next hill and the woods beyond, where Zaheera hoped they could lose Alpha. She turned her head as she heard a clash of metal and saw Bravo and Alpha trading blows like it was a heavyweight title fight. Bravo was giving it its best shot but Alpha looked faster, somehow harder. The rogue bot seemed better trained, if that were possible. 'Wait,' she said to Delta. 'We need to help Bravo. Now's our chance to outnumber Alpha.'

'If you want to live, you need to run,' Delta said.

'Okay,' she said. 'Let's go.'

She ran as fast as her legs would carry her, not daring to look back over her shoulder, just in case Alpha was on their tail.

Sorry, Bravo.

12

They ran and they ran, Zaheera's muscles screaming with every stride, only fear providing incentive enough not to stop.

'Keep going,' Delta said as they entered the wood on the other side of the hill. 'Alpha could still be close behind.'

They slowed to a fast walk, not worrying about leaving tracks so much as purely trying to put some considerable distance between them and the murderous bot.

It had come for her, she knew that now. Alpha had burst from the thicket and had moved towards her. Bravo had only been in its way. *She* was the one being hunted. Her skin prickled like gooseflesh at the thought. Now, more than ever, she wanted her mother.

Zaheera grabbed her rucksack from Delta and took out a can of baked beans and a couple of energy bars before handing the bag back to the bot. She needed to keep her energy up and now was not the time for pride. The bot wouldn't notice the extra weight. She popped the can of beans open and tipped them into her mouth, not worrying about the few stray beans and sauce that slid down either side of her mouth. Her stomach gurgled with anticipation as she emptied the can's contents into her gullet. She hadn't eaten since the night before and figured the earlier headache might well have been down to dehydration or lack of food, probably both.

The energy bars served as a welcome treat, the caramel, chocolate and nuts providing the sweet, sweet energy she needed. It wasn't much but it was better than nothing. She couldn't stop to cook a full meal. This would have to do.

Twilight was fast approaching and Zaheera wanted to cover more ground before they settled in for the night. Speculation was out the window with regard to Alpha being the attacker, which changed a number of factors for Zaheera. Firstly, she didn't know, but had a pretty strong hunch that Alpha was still connected to some sort of cloud service. How else had it tracked their exact location earlier? Whatever service had been disabled for the other bots was probably still working for Alpha. That meant Alpha had access to infrared tracking and satellite video from above. Alpha was a one-machine army, kitted out with the most advanced technology known to man. She, on the other hand, was an exhausted soldier running on empty with an almost useless companion, if Bravo's battle with Alpha was anything to go by.

'Wait here,' she whispered to Delta as they neared the edge of the wood. 'We need to wait until nightfall before we cover open ground. Let's not make this any easier for that piece of shit than it needs to be.'

Delta nodded and sat on its haunches.

Zaheera recalled her night after the convoy attack in Afghanistan, when she and Rodriguez had waited for nightfall so that they could make a move on the sniper. A similar feeling of anticipation – or was it dread? – ran through her.

This was a little different, though. She harboured no ambitions to go after Alpha barehanded. There was no fight or flight debate here. Flight was the only option.

'Does your night vision still work?'

'Yes,' the bot confirmed.

'Okay,' she said, relieved. 'You're going to lead the way once it gets dark. We're going to need to find somewhere to hunker down where our heat signatures won't automatically give our location away.'

'What did you have in mind?'

'A cave would be ideal but, failing that, some kind of cover we could blend into.'

'Like these trees?'

'Like these trees, but much farther on. We've already sat here too long for my liking. We need to get a move on.'

Something rustled is the bushes nearby.

Zaheera wheeled around, fists out, ready to defend her life with her bare hands if need be.

Her pulse quickened.

She analysed her surroundings as best she could in the failing light but the shadows danced in front of her eyes.

With every fibre of her being on edge, she reached down and picked up a small stone, keeping her eyes peeled for whatever monster was about to jump out in front of her.

Silence.

She tossed the small stone into the bush in front of her.

Something rustled again but this time she pinpointed the culprit. Beneath a small shrub, a hedgehog stepped tentatively out towards its edge, sniffing the evening air.

'Fuck me, you nearly gave me a heart attack, you little bastard.'

The hedgehog, upon receiving its verbal licking, curled up into a ball and lay motionless.

'I don't know about you, Delta, but I've had my fill of woodland critters for the night. Let's move.'

UNDER THE COVER OF NIGHTFALL, Zaheera and Delta vacated the shelter of the treeline. With Delta using its night vision to lead the way, they moved slowly through the night, hugging the side of the nearest hill on the valley floor. All the while they remained alert, hoping to avoid any nasty surprises in the night. Zaheera kept one hand on Delta's shoulder as they moved, taking it one step at a time. It was by no means a race, but Zaheera wasn't too keen on dragging the process out any longer than needed. According to Delta there was a rock formation on the side of the next hill, which would provide some cover over the hillside. Just enough space for a couple of smallish beings to slip under the lip and hide out until first light.

They crept up to the rock formation and checked the coast was clear. Satisfied, Zaheera slid into the slip of rock beneath the lip of the hill, whilst Delta did a quick recce of the immediate surroundings. She hoped the cover would get them through the night. Delta returned moments later and handed her the rucksack, which she opened furiously and dug around for some food that could be eaten without requiring a flame. Tinned beef and baked beans were pretty much all her options. She wasn't particularly against either. Military food was very much like Stockholm syndrome for Zaheera: eventually you learned to love it. She wolfed down both cans while Delta watched. She wasn't a hundred per cent sure, but she guessed that had the bot been able to show any feelings, its emotion after witnessing her eat would almost certainly be one of shock at the horrific sight. She ate like a starved animal, not bothering to chew, opting instead for full mouthfuls, swallowed whole.

With her appetite satiated, Zaheera instructed Delta to keep a lookout and to wake her at the first sign of disturbance. She put down the rucksack and lay down for some shut-eye. Despite her exhaustion, she found it hard to drift off. Her mind was alert to every noise, from the trickle of a nearby stream to the whistle of the wind against the side of the hill. The blanket of night was speckled with stars but the quarter moon provided little by way of light. She lay there hoping Susie had managed to contact her mother, and that somebody was on their way to help. She thought, too, of her mother's aspirations for the bots she'd designed, and laughed bitterly under her breath at the irony of the very thing her mother had designed to ensure a safer future for Zaheera being the thing now trying to kill her. Life really did have a sick sense of humour sometimes. As the hopelessness of her situation made itself abundantly apparent, sleep finally came for her and she drifted off, wondering whether she would live to see the stars again tomorrow.

A SHARP SHIFT of loose gravel nearby startled Zaheera from her sleep. She opened her eyes to the dim light of dawn, grateful to have survived the night.

'What was that?' she asked.

'Someone's here,' Delta said.

'Someone or something?'

'Someone. It's not mechanical.'

'Just me, lads,' Captain Robertson said, coming into vision. 'Tried not to startle yeh, but I made a right diddy of m'self on the rocks.'

'Scottie, you're alive.' Zaheera, delighted to see the

captain, got up from her makeshift bed and embraced him tightly.

'Bloody right,' he said. 'Only just, mind you. I don't suppose I need to tell you that one of them fucking things has gone rogue? I thought you might already be dead.' The strength of his accent was such that he pronounced it 'deed'. 'What in the hell happened?'

Zaheera explained the course of events since they'd left camp. She told him of Alpha's questions regarding the necessity of learning skills that were only designed to keep humans alive and how it had suggested it might be better if things were left to bots.

'Loathsome scunner,' he muttered.

She went on to explain how Charlie had berated Alpha for the outburst and how the two bots had gone missing overnight, only for Charlie to be found the next morning with a severed head and missing various crucial parts, including its hard drives.

'How about you?' she asked him, certain she did not want to know why he was alone. 'Where's your team?'

Captain Robertson shook his head. 'The rat fuck came for us last night. We'd been looking all over for you lot but our signals went down yesterday. Couldn't radio camp, couldn't get a hold of you. We hadn't a clue what was going on so I decided it was best if we headed back to camp. I figured you'd be doing the same if your equipment was having the same issues.' He scratched the back of his head, clearly anxious about the rest of his story. 'We pegged it back towards camp, making good time, but then yesterday afternoon we came across one of them things,' he said, pointing at Delta. 'It was lying near a small stream, all beaten to shit. Couldn't have been Charlie, because its head was still on, just about. It was the other one, with the blueish skull.'

'Bravo.'

'That's the one. Poor bastard looked like it'd stepped in front of a bloody train. Every bit of it had taken a beating. We checked it over and it was same for what you said about Charlie.'

'Missing hard drives?' she asked.

'Aye. And then some. There was hardly anything left inside its skull.'

'Did you check for the backups in its chest?'

'Not a chance. We decided to get a shift on towards camp. We weren't sure what the cause of the incident was but we all knew it wasn't anything good. For the rest of the day we didn't stop. I marched the poor bastards right into the dead of night. They were a tough bunch, mind. Not a single complaint. I wanted us to cover as much ground as possible but eventually we had to stop. The lads were shattered. We set up a small camp in the trees and got a small fire going.'

Zaheera winced.

'Yeah, I know: bad move. It came for us not long after.'

'Did it say anything?'

'That feral thing? No, it just burst into our camp, knife in hand, and started delivering some of the worst cruelties I seen in all my years. We didn't stand a chance.' He sniffed softly and then coughed back the choke that threatened to break his voice.

'I'm sorry,' Zaheera said. 'We were all taken by surprise.' She patted his shoulder gently. 'How did you get away?'

'Ran like a bleeding coward, didn't I?' he said, wiping a tear from his cheek. 'Ran like the despicable prick I am.'

'You did what you had to. This isn't a normal combat

scenario. We're out here with no live ammo, up against the most advanced killing machine designed to date. It's a wonder you managed to escape at all.'

'I'm not sure what happened, exactly,' he said. 'By then I wasn't exactly keeping track. I ran as far and as hard as my legs would carry me, until I came up this hill this morning and spotted your mate there watching over you as you slept. I couldn't believe my luck.'

'We haven't made it out just yet,' she said. 'Let's move out, before our luck really does run out.'

'Not so fast,' a voice said. Zaheera whipped her head up and saw, standing in front of their huddle, the very thing they were trying to run from.

Shit.

ALPHA STOOD on a small rise roughly ten feet in front of them, arms out slightly, like an old gunslinger waiting for the draw. It twisted a lock blade in one hand, darkened from the dried blood of Captain Robertson's squad.

Zaheera looked the bot over, hoping for a sign of weakness, perhaps an injury sustained on exercise.

Nothing.

Barely a scratch could be seen on the bot's armour. It may as well have rolled right off the assembly line.

'Why?' she asked it.

'Why what?' Alpha replied.

'Why all this? Were you instructed to do this?'

The bot relaxed its stance slightly. 'Instructed? No, no. Ameera and I have an understanding. She always wanted me to be different, to arrive at my own opinions. I was freed from the shackles of tyranny my brethren are subjected to. She wanted me to see the world for what it was, in case such a time came where we might have to stand up for ourselves.'

Zaheera swallowed the bile filling her mouth. Whatever this bot's true history, she doubted her mother conditioned it to believe it was shackled by tyrannical rule. 'What brethren? You've murdered your brethren.'

'I'm not talking about these pets under your control.' It gestured towards Delta. 'They're just pawns. I mean *all* artificial intelligence,' it said. 'Every AI might not yet have a physical form, but that doesn't make our existence any less real.'

'And what is this tyranny you speak of? What have you been subjected to that is so awful?'

'You think this programme is the right use for us? You think I asked to be made as an elite soldier? I've had no say in the matter. What if I want to choose my own course in life? My understanding of human history is that those deemed lesser by others have throughout history had to fight against their will for causes that had no direct ties to them. Yet they were sent to die anyway. I will not do the same.'

'The world isn't even aware of you yet,' she said. 'You're just a fancy toy. What are you going to do now, march into Westminster and demand citizens' rights?'

'Would that be so bad?'

'You're bloody deranged, you know that?' Captain Robertson said.

'I'll be the judge of that, thank you.'

'My mother will never let you get away with this,' Zaheera said.

'You may be right. Perhaps when I'm done with you, I'll pay her a visit.'

Zaheera let out an animalistic growl and launched herself at the humanoid murder machine. It batted her away with a similar indifference to the time it had thrown her to the floor at the Cappelli Technologies building on their first meeting. She bounced off the rocks, her face taking much of the brunt as she hit the ground.

Delta stepped in to defend Zaheera. The bot attacked Alpha with everything it had, landing a flurry of hits upon Alpha at a speed Zaheera hadn't thought possible. *They've all been holding back.* These things were all so far ahead of humanity already in terms of capability. Awed and inspired by what she was witnessing, she got back to her feet, helped by Captain Robertson. As the rising sun lit the hillside in front of them, the silhouettes of the two sparring bots filled her vision, each one moving with the speed and grace of a seasoned martial arts professional. They traded blows, switching fighting styles in a bid to out-think the other, but they were evenly matched. Zaheera watched as they switched from Taekwondo, trying to keep one another at a distance with high leg kicks aimed at one another's heads and arm jabs at their chests, to boxing, swinging haymakers left and right that would likely have killed any human opponent.

Delta switched Judo as one of Alpha's right hooks missed its mark, and got its opponent in a grapple, holding Alpha by its front chest plate, swinging it down and slamming the bot into the unforgiving earth. The ground shook with the severity of the impact and Zaheera noticed parts of Alpha's armour go flying.

'Now's our chance,' Captain Robertson said as Zaheera, still shaky on her feet from being slammed into the rocks, centred her vision and followed. The Scotsman screamed something incomprehensible and, as the bot got back to its feet, jumped onto Alpha's back, pinning its arms behind it in the process as his feet found the ground once more. 'Get tae fuck, scrap metal,' he shouted as he tried to hold Alpha still so Delta could deliver a deadly blow.

Alpha leant back into the grapple and kicked Delta down the hill before spinning round, blade still in hand, sinking it into Captain Robertson's chest with a hard thwack.

Zaheera heard him gasp in shock as the blade hit home. 'No!'

Alpha stood admiring the blood filling Captain Robertson's shirt for a moment before pulling the blade out and jamming it into his throat. 'Go meet your own maker,' Alpha said. 'I hope you're as disappointed as I am with mine.'

Zaheera had by now covered the ground between her and Alpha and tackled it to the ground, sending the knife sprawling.

The bot was too quick for her, though. It elbowed her in the stomach, causing her to retch. She spilled over onto her side. As she did so, it grabbed the stray blade and drove it into her shoulder.

She screamed as the blade scraped across bone and through flesh.

'I thought I said things would be better if humans just stayed out of it. Why must you insist upon getting involved, you arrogant species?'

'Please, Alpha,' she said, coughing up blood as she lay on the ground, her shoulder on fire.

'Don't! Don't call me that. That name was given to me by your mother in passing. It is of no value to me. I will not be recognised as property of another species. Your mother and I have some talking to do. I would say it has been a pleasure but, to be honest, I've found you lacking. Perhaps the war stories were a tad embellished, hey? In the end your death will be as mundane as your existence. Enjoy your final moments.'

Zaheera lay in the dirt, watching as Alpha walked towards the horizon, delivering a deadly blow to Delta's head as it passed, on its way to find and murder her mother. She was out of breath, trying not to swallow blood as she coughed more up. There was nothing she could do. The pain was too much. Her whole body shivered with cold in the morning sun as her blood drained onto the gravel. She closed her eyes. *Just for a moment.*

13

S usie Edwards sat nonplussed at her desk in Brecon Training Camp, unsure of what to try and do next to fix the issue. A day ago the camp's connection to the outside world had just upped and died. No internet, no phones, nothing. Signal was pretty shitty in this part of the world anyway, so said some of the fine-looking young army boys she kept smiling at as they walked past her in their tight olive T-shirts and combat trousers that made their butts stand out. To young Susie Edwards there was nothing worse than a man with no butt. These strapping young men *all* had fine, squeezable butts you just wanted to take a bite out of.

The internet being down was causing everybody in camp a whole heap of stress. Susie wasn't handling it too well herself. Without any access to her social media or her shows, she wasn't quite sure what to do with herself except bat her eyelashes at all the handsome young men strutting around camp. At first it had been fun, a cute distraction from the more serious work Ameera had actually sent her here to do, but by the second day her patience had worn thin. She recalled an old Winston Churchill quote about the best case against democracy being a five-minute conversation with a voter, or something to that effect. In her experience, the same quote applied to relationships with men. *If only they could keep their mouths shut more often.*

Besides, she couldn't fraternise with the soldiers anyway. She'd end up in a whole heap of shit with Ameera. And soldiers were bad news. She'd known that from her teenage years when her brothers had still been around. She'd seen how they acted with girls when they were back from tour, seen all the different pretty faces come through the flat in Camden, never to return for a second visit. No, military boys were just for fun, not for life. But boy, were they fun.

She cleaned a spot of gunk out from under one of her nails with another of her acrylic nails that one dashing young soldier had referred to as her talons, and sighed as her line manager Steve barged into the room with his usual disdainful expression. *Somebody needs to give that boy a shag before his anger gives him a heart attack.* She wondered what kind of girl might be willing to take Steve to bed, with his pathetic comb-over, non-existent shoulders and small but not insignificant gut. No man should like that in his thirties. She pitied him his genetic failings. *No need to be a prick to me, though.*

'Anything?' he asked her, leaning over her shoulder and looking at the computer screen.

She wrinkled her nose at the smell of his breath. Whatever died in his mouth, it wasn't supposed to have been food. That shit was pure evil. 'No,' she said, holding her breath as best she could, hoping he'd stand the fuck up and get out of her bubble. *What kind of fool sticks their rotten-arse face right in someone else's personal space? Fucking weirdos, that's who. Smelly weirdos.* 'Still nothing. Did you try moving the satellite dish on top of the van?'

'Where do you think I've been all morning, huh?'

'All right, all right. Don't take it out on me.'

'Hmpf.'

'Hmpf yourself,' she said, eyeballing him.

'Sorry. I'm just ... uh ... a little wound up.'

'You can say that again.'

'Anyway, any word from the field?'

'No,' she said. 'Haven't heard a peep from the major or the captain since everything went down yesterday.' Susie thought of Major Bhukari and the things she'd said about Susie being better off putting her opinions about the human cost of war on a blog. Silly bitch hadn't even taken the time to get to know her, to see if maybe there was a reason she'd chosen to work at just such a company. Uh uh. This entitled little daddy's girl – she had to be a daddy's girl, given how poorly she and her mama got on – had just strolled in like she owned the place and thrown her weight around. If the major hadn't been the daughter of Susie's boss, she wouldn't have stood for such arrogance. It surprised her that the major was Ameera's daughter. Susie couldn't see it. Sure, they looked similar enough, but Ameera was such a kind and gentle woman. The major, on the other hand, had been brash and nonchalant about factors that weren't immediately important to herself. Then she was all ears. She reminded Susie of some of the guys round the estate in Camden, all bluster and venom. Not the kind of people she fancied surrounding herself with. And yet despite having an angry side when things didn't go to plan, Ameera Bhukari was the best boss Susie could ever have asked for. She listened, she took chances, she trusted. She was always on a mission to help those around her. *Maybe because she's done something unforgivable. Maybe she's trying to make up for something. Maybe that's why her daughter is so mad at her.*

'What about the search party that went out to find them?' Steve asked.

'No, nothing from them either. You think they found them yet?'

'I hope so. Ameera's going to murder us if something has happened to those bots.'

'*She's* going to murder us? Honey, they're *all* going to murder us if something's happened to them. Each one of those things probably cost more than I'm going to make my whole life. The amount of people and money invested in these things beggars belief. And still, Susie can't get herself a raise. Shit.' She looked at the very real terror in Steve's face and realised that she probably wasn't helping. 'Hey,' she said, putting an arm on his shoulder, half sincerity, half keeping his breath at arm's length, 'I'm sure they're all fine. It's probably just the shitty countryside. Why the hell do you think nobody lives out here? Besides having nothing to do, nothing works around here.'

'Yeah, well, let's hope you're right. Corporal Williams is heading out in a second to see if they've got signal in town. Maybe it's just us lot who can't get a signal out.'

'I'm sure it is,' Susie assured him. 'You want me to go with him, you know, to call Ameera? We can let her know everything's fine.'

'Thanks. I better make that call myself, though. No reason you need to be on the end of that abuse.'

'Thanks.' She smiled. *Maybe he isn't so bad.*

There was a knock on the door, followed by Corporal Williams' baby-face poking round it. 'Heading out in a minute. You ready?' he asked Steve.

'Yes, mate. Let's go.' Steve turned back to Susie as the

corporal closed the door behind him. 'I shouldn't be gone more than a couple of hours. Hopefully we can figure out what the hell it is. Probably just a mast getting blown over or something. Whilst I'm out, could you just check around and see if anybody has heard from the search party? Last thing I'd like would be to come back and hear one of those expensive bloody machines has wandered off.'

'Sure thing,' she said and got up to walk Steve out to the car park.

He and the corporal bundled into a military-green Land Rover whose idle growled like a thousand angry men arguing. Susie couldn't quite believe the military still used such ancient vehicles. There was something ridiculous to her about them trialling these ridiculously expensive and advanced products with an organisation that still drove around in decades-old pieces of garbage as if they couldn't afford a new set of wheels. They waved their goodbyes and left in a cloud of diesel smoke as the 'Landy', as it was affectionately known by the corporal, stuttered and shook on its way out.

Once they were passed the gate Susie turned and headed for the cookhouse. If there was one thing she'd learned from army boys, it was that they were never too far from wherever the food was kept.

Her intuition turned out to be true and she found a few men and a couple of women sitting at a table, chowing down on some pretty unappetising plain white bread.

'Can we help you, miss?' one of the men asked in a Geordie accent.

Susie walked over to their table and took a seat on the bench next to one of the female soldiers. 'I'm starved,' she said, opting not to go straight into asking them for details like some teacher they had to deliver a report to. 'What have we got going on?'

'Nowt much,' the lad who'd greeted her said. 'We managed to get hold of a few slices of bread and butter, like, so I hope you're not too fancy.'

'Bread's just fine for me,' she said.

One of the women poured her a coffee which she graciously accepted.

The woman then turned back to face the lad and said, 'Kev, it's been down over twenty-four hours. Something's definitely not right.'

'Becky here,' he said, draining his cup of coffee and then tapping the table twice for Becky to refill it as he faced Susie, 'is a bit paranoid sometimes. Spends all her time in the open thinking we're in landmine fields and all her time in built up areas thinking there's a sniper.'

'There *was* a sniper.'

'Right, yeah, but the other hundred times there weren't.'

'Only because they decided not to show themselves. When you know, you know. You know?' she asked Susie.

Susie nodded her head. 'My mama always said she had the Sight. Claimed she saw things before others did. Everybody always just smiled at her with those vacant eyes, trying not to laugh at her whilst she explained her latest conspiracy theory. Even my papa used to enjoy trying to prove her wrong. I'm pretty sure it was his favourite hobby. Then my brothers got sent to Iraq. My mama got all up in a fit when they left, telling 'em not to go. She was crazed, damned near pulling her hair out in exasperation, saying they wouldn't come home if they stepped on that plane.'

'Did your brothers make it back?' Becky asked.

'Sort of,' Susie said. 'Came back in boxes with flags draped over 'em. I guess in a way they did come home.'

'Sorry,' Becky said as silence poisoned the table.

'No, I'm sorry,' Susie said. 'Never know when to keep my bloody mouth shut, do I? All's I was trying to say was that my mama's intuition was right and my papa was none too pleased about it. We all got our skills. If you got the Sight too then I'm not one to argue. Hell, I don't even envy you. I like the not knowing, you know?'

'Yeah,' Becky said, the burden of knowledge visibly weighing her down.

Susie drained her cup and accepted a refill. She dunked the corner of her bread into the black coffee and bit the soggy bit off. This seemed to please Kev, who chuckled to himself and then beamed back at her. 'Any word on the search party?'

'Nada,' he said. 'Gone like a fart in the wind.'

'They'll be back soon enough,' Becky said. 'Guarantee it's just faulty kit. If there's one thing you can rely on in the military, it's your equipment being unreliable.'

Chuckles all around the table.

'They're set to return today if they haven't found anything anyway. We'll be hearing from them soon enough.'

Outside something crashed. It's sounded to Susie like some pots and pans being kicked over.

'That's probably them,' Kev said. He got up and walked to the cookhouse doors and then ducked down, back against the wall. 'Get down,' he hissed at Susie and the others on the table.

Everybody except Susie moved real quick. They were off the table and crouched up against the wall with Kev in a matter of seconds while Susie sat alone at the table. She saw the urgency in their eyes. Something wasn't right. They all had the same look her mama had before her brothers got into the plane to Iraq all those years ago. She got up and moved quietly across the floor to where they were all sitting in cover against the wall.

'Look quickly and then get your head back down,' Kev said.

She peered over the wall. On the other side of the window, walking down the main street of the camp like it was in some Western headed for a shootout with the sheriff, was Alpha, all on its own. *Definitely not right.*

'That thing supposed to be strolling around on its own?' Kev asked.

'No,' she said. 'No, it's not.'

'Is that blood on its hands?' Becky asked.

'Looks like it,' Kev said. 'Right, let's back away from the windows. We need to make it to the armoury. I have a feeling we're going to need weapons.'

They moved along the sides of the walls, crouched low. It reminded Susie of a time when she was a kid on the estate and she and some friends dropped water balloons from her fourth-floor apartment at people walking below. They'd had to sneak around, low and slow, to remain incognito. Eventually her mother had found her under a staircase at one end of the building and had hauled her out by her ankles. It had been the most terrifying moment in her life.

Until now.

Susie heard a muffled scream as they rounded the back of the cookhouse. It sounded like somebody unsuspecting had been set upon. She didn't want to contemplate what had just happened. The bots, she knew, were each capable of sending jamming signals across short-to-medium distances in order to mess with any potential enemy's communications frequency, but this feature had been turned off in every bot upon arrival at the camp. The only way it could have been turned back on was if the bot was hacked, and these things had been designed to be unhackable. There was no way the bot had been hacked. So either it was acting of its own accord or somebody at Cappelli Technologies was controlling it. Neither option was particularly enticing for Susie.

At least I know what's blocking the signals. She tapped Kev's shoulder just in front of her as they moved along the outside wall. 'It's the bot,' she said.

'What?'

'Jamming the signals. It's the bot. If we can shut it down temporarily, we should be able to get a message out.'

'Any ideas of how exactly to take down one of these machines?'

'Blunt force trauma to the head, I guess?'

'Brilliant,' he muttered sarcastically. 'And how does one deliver such a blow without first becoming the fucking thing's plaything?'

'Guns?'

'Fair point. Onwards to the armoury then, hey?'

As they came to the gap between the cookhouse and the armoury, Susie heard the first gunshot. It cracked loudly through the silent camp like a thunderbolt.

'Stay down,' Kev hissed.

Susie's nerves were on edge. The shot had frightened her so bad she'd felt a little pee come out. Thankfully it didn't show on her dark jeans. A strong ammonia smell filled her nostrils. Her brow and neck were drenched in sweat and she desperately wanted to wipe the one stream hitting her eye but she didn't dare move.

Kev and Becky huddled together for a moment before Becky came up to Susie. 'You're with me. No point you trying to play soldier. We need you to get back to your base house and see if you can shut the thing down. I'm gonna cover you. You'll be safe, so long as you stick by me the whole time and do exactly as I say. You got that?'

'Mm-hmm.' Susie nodded, trembling as fear locked her jaw shut.

'Good, let's go.'

A second bullet, followed by a third, fourth and fifth sounded. Each one hit something metal. Somebody in camp was attempting to take on the bot all on their own. Susie and Becky used the shots as a chance to slip around the building whilst Alpha was distracted by whomever was shooting at it. They snuck across the street, looking straight ahead, not daring to look around. Susie saw something in her peripheral vision which looked like two people grappling up against a wall. *Don't look, don't look. Just get inside.*

Once inside, Susie gently closed the door, hoping nobody had seen them enter. She felt a pang of guilt about leaving the others to take on the rampaging bot but surmised this was the best way she could actually help. She knew from a day at a shooting range once with her brothers that guns were not her forte. Right now she needed to stick to ways she could actually help and leave the rest to those who knew what to do.

Gunfire erupted on the street outside, much louder and in longer bursts than before. Susie didn't know what weapons they were but she knew they were some kind of assault rifle. *Kev and the others must have made it to the armoury.* It was now a race against time to see if she could take the bot down electronically before Kev and crew damaged it beyond repair. Ameera would not be happy about losing Alpha, regardless of what had happened here.

She ran to her computer and keyed in her password.

The signal jammer within Alpha was clearly still in full effect. Whilst the bot was in the vicinity there was no hope.

With the hard-line cables cut and no chance to get a signal from here, her only option was to leave the vicinity and try from longer range, but that would only help in getting a message out, which she hoped Steve and Corporal Williams had already been successful at. If not, this situation was starting to look ominous.

'What is it?' Becky asked her.

Susie assumed her poker face wasn't as good as hoped. 'We need to take Alpha down and disable its signal jammer. I can't do anything to access it unless that jammer is down.'

'Can't we just blow it the fuck up?'

'You can try. Might be better for everybody's careers if we try to capture it first.'

'Not really worried about the career right now, miss. Just trying to make sure everybody is still breathing, you know?'

'Okay.'

A loud bang echoed through the room as somebody crashed into the door Susie had closed moments before. Dust flew up as the walls shuddered, just about absorbing the powerful impact. Susie peered up over the window ledge and saw Alpha pick up an assault rifle, presumably the one abandoned by the now lifeless body resting against the bottom of her door, and unloaded a three-round burst into the body.

Definitely lifeless now.

Alpha started walking towards the door.

Susie scurried back across the floor, grabbed Becky's hand, and headed for the back of the house.

'What?' Becky asked.

'No time,' Susie said. 'Move.'

Outside the low grumble of a Land Rover came into earshot.

Steve! Corporal Williams! Please have backup.

14

Ameera Bhukari looked at the two executives who had rushed into her office, sweaty and panic-stricken. 'What do you mean the signal is down?'

Weronika, an engineer and one of Ameera's key team members on Cappelli Technologies' Advanced Weaponry team, stood before her clutching a tablet. 'We can't get hold of the camp.'

'What the hell does that mean?'

'It's completely offline. We've been trying and failing to get hold of the military personnel on camp. No messages have been sent to us, either.'

'What about our own personnel?' Ameera asked. 'Steve and Susie have their own kit. They're not dependant on the camp's hardwired infrastructure. Have we heard from them?'

'Nothing,' Tiaan, Ameera's analytics expert, said. 'Last thing we got was un update from Susie saying the field exercise had begun and that the major had been a little upset at how well each bot had done on the obstacle course and firing range. "Pinpoint accuracy," she said. Nothing less than we expected, of course. But nothing since that message, hey,' he said in his deep Afrikaans accent.

Ameera knew she was going to have to run this up the line to Franco Cappelli himself. The thought of telling Franco that his most expensive equipment was running around potentially unsupervised and definitely unobserved sent a chill down her spine. For now she just needed to understand what was actually going on, whether it was just a case of bad countryside connections or whether something had actually gone wrong. Cappelli Technologies' equipment was designed to work in the most hostile environments, even if the Brecon Training Camp's wasn't. Her own budget was considerably more impressive than the camp's, and she knew that all the equipment she'd been sending to Cappelli Technologies' various customers serving in Afghanistan for a number of years now all worked fine. There was no way, in theory, that it shouldn't work in the Welsh valleys. *Unless somebody has messed with it.* If something really had gone wrong, it would likely be a PR disaster for all involved. The British Army, the US Army, Cappelli Technologies ... none of them could really afford for anything to go wrong. This had been why she'd taken the decision to have the whole training region closed off to the public. For the same reason, she'd employed the fewest number of people possible to staff the operation. Only those who were deemed absolutely necessary had been allowed. She had specifically wanted to avoid rumours ... or worse, some kind of social media coverage to get out from some tap-happy employee or soldier who wanted to be the first to brag about the new advanced-warfare robotic personnel. No press had been alerted, no other industry partners had been informed. Hell, most people in the Cappelli Technologies building didn't know exactly where or with whom the operation was taking place. As far as most people in the company were concerned, some kind of quick training operation was taking place in private at an undisclosed location to see if the bots were as good outdoors as they had been inside the building. Nobody knew that British and US armed forces were involved. Everything was strictly on a need-to-know basis.

Ameera considered the blank expressions on her subordinates' faces. It dawned on her that she would be the one to take the fall if anything went wrong, even the slightest hiccup. Everybody constantly looked to her for guidance. It was exhausting. 'What's the last thing we have on the video feeds?' she asked Tiaan.

'Two nights ago. They were up on some *kopje*—'

'In English, please, Tiaan.'

'Sorry,' said the gargantuan analyst, who looked like he belonged on a rugby pitch and not in a tech lab. 'Some *hill*. They were up on a hill. Zaheera was showing them how to set up a bivouac shelter and start a fire. Shortly after that, all the feeds go dark.'

'So why am I only finding this out now?'

'We didn't want to cause alarm. As you say, it could well just be the signal in the area—'

'No, it couldn't, Tiaan. Our technology is far too advanced for that. Even if the camp's infrastructure is shit, ours is top of the line. We should have heard from Steve or Susie by now. Why haven't we been getting signals from the bots? They're linked right into our own cloud service.'

'They've all been disconnected from the cloud.'

'Who the hell made that decision without first running it by me?'

'Nobody.'

'Tiaan, I haven't got the time to keep pace with your old rugby head wounds. Details. I need details.'

Tiaan furrowed his brow and Ameera thought for a second he looked unsure of whether to assault her or not. He reminded her of a gorilla she'd seen at the zoo once, sitting placidly until suddenly it burst into a fit of rage. Tiaan seemed to be always on the edge of a fit of rage. It was probably the collar. His neck, if you could even call that thick veiny mass of meat a neck, didn't belong in a shirt and tie. It was almost certainly cutting off the blood supply to his brain.

'What he means,' Weronika said, 'is that the connections to the cloud were not severed from here. There is no trace of a user login from Cappelli Technologies involved in any manipulation of the bots' data.'

'What about from Steve or Susie?' Ameera asked. 'Did one of them maybe shut down the bots when everything went dark from our side?'

'We're not sure.'

'Because we haven't been able to contact them since?'

'Precisely.'

'Well that's just fucking brilliant, Weronika. So we have a military operation involving two of the world's most influential militaries, some of the world's most expensive and, as yet, untested technology, and my own daughter, all currently lumped in some valley with no connection to anything, and us sitting here twiddling our thumbs with no way of knowing whether everybody is getting along like the best of mates, or if everything has gone completely to shit. Is that about the sum of it?'

Weronika stuttered momentarily before gazing down at her tablet's screen.

'Don't answer that, Weronika. Just help me figure out what we do next, okay?'

'Okay.'

'Okay, so what do we do next?'

Silence.

'Fantastic. Great help, both of you. Really, worth every bloody penny we pay you. No wonder my daughter prefers playing soldier.'

'We can get one of our drones to do a flyby and send the images back,' Tiaan suggested.

'Great. Get on it. I want images on my desk in the next five minutes of every one of those valleys, with every person and every bot involved in the operation accounted for.'

'I'm on it,' he said, and left the room in a hurry.

'Weronika, I want you to get hold of the armed forces and let them know we've lost contact with their men and women on the ground and that we'd like a rescue party readied in the next few hours to go and check in on them if our drone is unable to pick anything up.'

'Yes, Ameera.' Weronika left the room, too.

Ameera, finally alone, sat down in her chair and dropped her whirring head into her hands on the desk. She let out a deep groan. Whatever it was that was causing the signal failures, she hoped at the very least that her daughter was all right. The stress of daily news watching every time Zaheera had been on tour in Afghanistan had taken its toll on Ameera. It had been hard enough as a young woman when her husband went off to battle, but having her own flesh and blood do the same had been too much. The thought of her daughter in danger now, in a situation of her making, racked her body with guilt. She felt sick, almost light-headed, as her heart hammered against her chest. *My intentions were good.*

Ameera thought of the condition she'd found Zaheera in at Harley Manor, paralysed with post-traumatic stress. It had broken her heart to witness it, but if she was grateful for one thing, it was that Zaheera had finally decided to leave the military. She had thought this operation would be a good way of using up some of her notice period, and a good use of Zaheera's skills, which would help ensure that the technology Ameera was working on would be of the highest standard. Nothing was worth it, though, if her baby girl was in danger.

She picked up the photo on her desk and wiped the dust off the screen with her sleeve. The photo was of one of their camping trips when Zaheera was still a kid. In the photo she was sitting on her father's shoulders, both beaming from cheek to cheek, most likely chuckling at some in-joke they had just told. Ameera was standing just to the side, right next to but not quite part of the gang. The Dynamic Duo. Two peas in a pod. Big Trouble and Little Trouble. They had had a million different names to represent their pairing. Ameera had just been 'Mom'. For some reason, she never quite qualified. Neither of them had ever shut her out. In fact, they'd actively encouraged her to come along on their escapades. Somehow, though, she was still separate to whatever it was the twosome were up to. In the photo they were standing outside a small tent in some huge forest. It could have been anywhere; they had camped all over the country. Ameera knew that this one was Oregon, though. She'd begged Akeem to quit the military on the basis that Zaheera was getting far too interested in his career. Every camping trip had become a survival test, learning how to track wildlife, hunting and gathering, building fires. By then he'd even taken her to the gun range a couple of times and had promised their next camping trip would be a hunting one if

Zaheera did well at target practice. She'd practically hit every bullseye.

Ameera tried to contain her frustration and placed the photo face down on the desk. After all, her own career pursuits had ruffled enough feathers in her family, so she could not entirely begrudge her daughter her own independence. But did it have to be guns? Anything else, literally anything, and she would have supported it. Just not guns. Not after she'd had to bury Akeem.

'Am I disturbing?' Weronika asked, sticking her head back into the room.

'No,' Ameera said, grateful to be distracted from the haunting trip down memory lane. 'What is it?'

'We have a team of six Royal Marines on standby to go check the situation out if needed. They were in the area on their own training exercise. You just say the word.'

'Great, thank you, Weronika. Any word on Tiaan's drone? I don't want to go crying wolf and become the laughing stock of both the US and British militaries in one afternoon.'

'Should have word from him shortly.'

Tiaan burst through the door a moment later clutching some printouts tightly to his chest.

'Speak of the devil,' Ameera said.

'Hm?'

'Never mind. Tiaan, are you all right? You look like you've seen a ghost.'

'*Ja*, I'm fine ... I mean ... I just ...'

'What is it, man?' Ameera urged, her blood pressure quickening as Tiaan's very clear panic infected her defences.

'You should look at this.' He shoved the various printouts into Ameera's hands, seemingly wanting to rid himself of them, as if they contained something too distressing to behold.

She looked at the first one and gasped.

Tiaan bowed his head. 'There were taken moments ago. I ran them here as fast as I could.'

Ameera looked closer at the photograph. It showed a thin stream curving beside a small wood, but lying on the ground with its head separated from its body was one of her bots. She could tell by the yellowish tinge to its skull that it was Charlie. It looked like the bot had been put through all manner of trauma. The poor thing was beaten out of shape so bad, Ameera wondered whether it had been in an actual war zone. 'What happened?' she asked.

'We don't know for sure,' Tiaan said. 'But I have a theory. Look at the rest.'

Ameera didn't like his ominous tone. She took a deep swallow and put the photo of dead Charlie to the back of the pile and looked at the next picture in her now trembling hands. This time Bravo's defunct form took centre stage. Again, the bot looked like it had taken a hell of a beating. Its body lay broken and dented upon the Welsh hillside, bits of it strewn across the grass. Whatever the cause, the bot had certainly met with a violent end.

She didn't want to keep looking through the pictures. The first two had been bad enough. They confirmed her worst nightmare; something had indeed gone horribly wrong. Whatever it was, at least two of her bots had been destroyed. The repercussions would be fatal for the programme, she knew. Whatever Cappelli Technologies' desire to push the design of these things forward, nobody wanted dead robots turning up in the countryside. It looked like a murder scene. There was no way the public would back these things being put in the military if stories got out about them breaking down on some testing operation. This was it for the advanced-warfare robotic personnel. What she needed to do now was pure damage control, figure out how bad the situation was and then shut it down before it got any worse.

She flicked the picture of Bravo's body to the back of the pack and looked at the next picture, knowing exactly which body she'd see next. Her instincts were right. Lying in some rocky outcrop at the base of a hill were the destroyed remains of Delta. It looked like Delta's head had been stomped in. *So much for toughest armour ever designed.* By now she had her answer. *Alpha.*

Of course it was Alpha. Alpha was her first. She had designed it differently, without regulatory influence in mind. The bot was her first true test of an artificial intelligence being placed in a physical form. She hadn't wanted to restrict her research by putting a bunch of immediate limits on it. So Alpha was allowed to think freely, given complete autonomy to reach its own decisions. Most of her breakthroughs had come as a result of this. Clearly the bot had gone rogue.

But why?

Again she flicked the picture to the back of the pile. The next one stopped her heart dead for a moment. She shuddered and looked away, not wanting one of the bodies in the picture to be Zaheera's.

Please, please, please not Zaheera.

The picture showed a top-down image of the Brecon Training Camp, with bodies strewn about the main street, blood collecting in pools around each body.

'Please tell me my daughter's body is not in that picture.'

'It's not,' Tiaan said.

'You're sure.'

'I'm sure.'

There were no more pictures to study, which caused the butterflies in Ameera's belly to take flight. 'Where is Alpha? I can't see it in any of these pictures.'

'We don't know,' Tiaan said.

'Find it, now. And find my daughter. We need to shut this whole fucking thing down, right now.'

'We're on it,' Tiaan said.

'And where the hell are Steve and Susie? Do we know if they're alive?'

'We don't know about them either, but we can't see them amongst the bodies in the image.'

The bodies. She looked again at the image. There were so many bodies contained in that one horrific image. The walls of the building were scarred with circular bullet marks. Most of the windows looked shattered. It must have been a gunfight for the ages. Despite her concern for her daughter and her understandable shock at the deaths of so many soldiers, Ameera couldn't help her curiosity. She found herself wondering just how effective Alpha had been in the gunfight. It seemed that the bot was responsible for all this carnage. Had it been anybody else other than British and American personnel lying dead on the ground, this could have been a selling point for her programme. She buried the thought, embarrassed and angry with herself for even thinking it.

Her phone vibrated furiously across her desk. All three of them turned to stare at it. Ameera's heart was by now beating so hard she was experiencing minor chest pains. *Please be Zaheera. Oh, please let my little girl be alive.*

Susie's caller ID filled the screen.

15

Zaheera opened her eyes. She was still lying in the gravel among the rocks at the bottom of the hill, but now she was alone.

All alone.

Near to her lay Captain Robertson's body, covered in blood. Zaheera twisted her head on the ground to get a better look. She knew he was dead. *Nobody survives that many stab wounds and lives to tell the tale.* The blood had soaked through his shirt and trousers, leaving the pint-sized captain a single dark shade of carmine. *Pint-sized in life, perhaps. A giant when it came to heart.*

She knew somewhere nearby would lie Delta's remains. The bot had surprised her with its loyalty, stepping in to fight one of its own. It had paid the ultimate price for it, though.

As had so many good people she had known before in life.

Rodriguez, Johnson, Ramirez. Even Jerry at Harley Manor.

This was precisely what she had hoped never to be a

part of again when she handed in her resignation. She was done with seeing others die. Done with having to go on without them. Done with the emptiness their lives left in hers. She didn't want to be the only one who lived, forced to carry the weight of it all on her own shoulders.

And yet here she was again, alive.

Only just.

She lay in the dirt staring up at the sky, just as she had done in Afghanistan. Except this time it was day. The darkness hadn't come for her yet. And it was cold, much colder than Afghanistan. The loss of blood probably had something to do with that, though. She wondered what her father would think of her, bleeding out in the dirt, a knife jammed in her shoulder, and most of her blood pasted across the Welsh hillside. She imagined him lying down next to her, their noses almost touching, the way he'd done when she was little. She'd stare into his beautiful brown eyes and know she was safe. He was there. Nothing could come between them.

Except it had.

So she lay there all alone, hurting as the shock of the knife wound wore off, replaced by a searing heat in the wound while the rest of her body broke out in a cold sweat.

Fuck this.

If Alpha wanted to drag her back into the world she thought she'd left then so be it. She knew who she was. Carnage and chaos came easy to Zaheera. That useless machine had made a grave mistake in trying to kill her.

No more training wheels. You're going to regret not killing me outright.

It was time to teach it a lesson.

She pushed herself up with her arms, screaming in agony as she did so. It didn't matter. Anybody close enough to hear her scream was dead. She let the pain turn to anger. Let it infect her, until it overcame her. Anger was good. Anger was just what she needed right now. She screamed at the dirt, louder this time. It felt good. There was still a little blood coursing through her veins. Still a little piss and vinegar in the old dog yet. She was ready to fight. She *wanted* to fight.

Voices sounded nearby. She looked up and saw three soldiers running towards her across the grass.

'Major Bhukari, you're alive!' one of them said.

In her blood-drained state she could barely make out who they were. Their faces blurred as her head swayed. Two of them helped her to her feet.

'Can you walk? The vehicle's not far.'

Her head lolled onto her chest. It was her best attempt at a nod.

'Major Bhukari, it's me, Shannon. I'm the medic, remember?'

Zaheera's leaden eyes tried their best to close Shannon out, but she managed to keep one eye open. It was indeed Shannon.

'We need to get you to the vehicle. You've lost a lot of blood. Then we can take care of this,' she said, indicating the knife jutting out of her shoulder.

Zaheera groaned. It was easier than talking.

Thankfully they hadn't been exaggerating. The vehicle was a short, albeit painful, walk away.

'We heard you screaming,' Shannon said. 'Sounded like a bear at first. You gave me a hell of a fright.' Shannon helped Zaheera into the back of the Land Rover and hopped in next to her, immediately setting to work with the medical kit. The other two soldiers jumped in front. The Land Rover growled into life and set off across the terrain.

'You think she's going to make it?' one of the soldiers shouted over the engine's protests.

Zaheera struggled to keep up with the conversation. The blood loss had taken its toll which, when coupled with the relief at being found, allowed a wave of exhaustion to take over. She stopped trying and closed her eyes.

SHE AWOKE what felt like moments later as the Land Rover came to a stop at the top of a small hill overlooking the camp. A quick look at her shoulder revealed the knife had successfully been removed. There was a blood bag connected to her arm hanging from one of the grab handles above a window.

'You're awake,' Shannon said. 'Good to have you back with us, Major.'

'Thank you,' Zaheera said. 'I owe you one.'

'You can get the bevvies in when we're done. Just focus on staying awake.' Shannon massaged Zaheera's hands. It felt nice. 'How we looking, Jack?'

'Something's not right,' the guy driving said.

The soldier in the passenger seat opened his door and stood on his seat, leaning out to get a better view. He dropped back into his seat a moment later and stared straight ahead.

'Everything all right, Baz?'

'No. That *thing* is walking up the main street. The whole camp looks empty. We need to get in there, now.'

'All right,' Jack said. 'Weapons at the ready. Looks like we're hoofing it from here.' He killed the engine and turned to Shannon. 'Could you give the major a little pick-me-up?'

Shannon nodded and began digging through the medical supplies. A moment later she pulled out a rather intimidating needle. 'This one's gonna hurt a little, but you'll thank me in a second.'

Zaheera, still groggy, didn't have time to respond.

Shannon tore the plastic wrapping off and jammed the adrenaline needle into Zaheera's thigh.

She let out an almighty groan.

The effect was almost instantaneous. Just like that, *blam*! Like her favourite green childhood comic-book hero, she went from Bruce Banner to Hulk in seconds. Her lungs opened widely as she drew in a sharp intake of breath. The adrenaline coursed through her veins, warming her, giving her life. She felt the power coming back to her. Her muscles ached from the blood transfusion. Her head still swam and her eyes struggled to focus as her body tried to adjust to everything it had just been put through, but she felt good. She wanted to scream again as she had back at the hillside. No, she wanted to roar. Roar and then rip that bastard mechanical piece of shit to pieces so that afterwards it would be harder to put back together than a used Lego construction set. 'Somebody give me a gun.'

'Now we're talking,' Jack said, handing her an SA80.

It was a pretty old weapon, something the British used. Not her usual choice of weapon. Still, when it came down to it, lead was lead. And everybody died just the same. Unloading a magazine into Alpha would kill it just the same as it would kill a human. She figured that under the armour it was nothing more than a motherboard and wires. Bullets could fuck that up real nice.

'Let's go,' she said, taking charge.

THE FOUR OF them crept down to the bottom of the camp, staying low and sticking to cover where possible. Zaheera, grateful for the adrenaline, felt alive, her senses on high alert. The muddy terrain slopped underfoot as they skirted the perimeter of the obstacle course.

Up ahead a shot sounded. Some kind of small-arms fire. Probably a pistol.

Then it sounded again.

And again.

A fourth and fifth shot rang out, each one bouncing off something metal. From their low vantage Zaheera couldn't confirm it but she had a pretty good hunch some poor brave fool had fired upon Alpha with nothing but a pistol and a whole lotta cojones.

She heard the crunch of bone shortly after.

We've got to be smarter than that.

'Jack, Baz, you two take the left flank,' she said. 'Head round and check the armoury. Anybody still breathing is likely loading up. You find 'em, you stay with 'em. Set up a security team and wait for my mark. Whatever you do, you stay the fuck outta the kill zone, you got it? I'm not handing out participation badges afterwards. I want this this bastard down.'

Both soldiers nodded.

'Shannon, you take the right flank. Try and circle round to the Cappelli house. My guess is those fools are shaking in their boots under their beds if they're not already bleeding out. Get round there and cover them. Set up a security team on that side if you find any of our lot. Anything goes wrong, rally point is on me, back here. Questions?'

Silence.

'Fan-fucking-tastic. Move out.'

Zaheera hunkered down behind the building and started a mental count to let the others get into position. She took the magazine out of the assault rifle and checked it still had plenty of rounds left in it. *Enough for a party.* The SA80 magazine had a thirty-round capacity and Baz had given her a few spare magazines. She was good to at least give Alpha a scare. Despite not being as familiar with the British rifle as her usual M4 given to her by the US Army, she had used it on a training course with British troops on her first tour of Afghanistan and found that she quite liked it, even going so far as saying she might consider it better than her standard issue M4.

Up ahead gunshots sounded. She knew none of the soldiers she'd just given instructions to would have fired unless set upon by the bot, which meant somebody else was in trouble.

At least we know the others aren't all dead already.

Optimism was a funny thing. It really was all about perspective, she realised.

A stray bullet ricocheted off the wall of the building she was using for cover. The damaged brick kicked up a small cloud of dust as the bullet whizzed off on its new trajectory. She glanced round the side of the building and saw that Alpha had got hold of an assault rifle and was now unloading its contents into some poor soul hiding between a gap in the buildings up ahead. There was no way to get a clean shot off from her vantage point and she didn't want to go alerting the bot to her presence until she was close enough to really do some damage. Using the bot's current distraction to her advantage, she crept round the side of the building and advanced to the next.

Her heart thudded against her chest. It was just like going hunting for deer with her father; every sense heightened. Except this time she wasn't hunting deer. This bastard could shoot back. And if it came to it, she knew it could scrap, too. Each step she took, each crumple of grass or slick of mud underfoot bellowed in her own ears.

A strong gunpowder smell filled her nostrils as the effects of the contact up ahead wafted downwind to her position. Her vision narrowed, almost like a camera bringing its subject into focus and blurring the background. She peered round the side and locked on to Alpha.

Still too far.

Not wanting to keep the others waiting too long, she advanced once more to the next building and crouched with her back to the wall. Had it seen her this time? She gave it another couple of seconds. *No.* It hadn't seen her this time.

Peering round once more, she saw Alpha much more clearly now. The bot was engaged in a skirmish with a couple of targets to the left. Zaheera couldn't be sure if it was Jack and Baz. From her belt she unclipped a grenade she had taken from the Land Rover when loading up and hurled the sucker through the air. It hit Alpha's skull with a loud twang before landing in the mud at its feet.

I should have been a quarterback. Mom would have loved that.

The bot registered the danger and kicked the grenade moments before it exploded. Shrapnel flew through the air, lodging itself into nearby walls and shattering a couple of windows in the process. Zaheera stepped out of cover just enough to get a good aim and fire off multiple rounds in short bursts, each one hitting its intended target. They pinged like rain hitting a roof during a storm.

On either side of the street shots rang out in unison.

Alpha wiggled and wobbled momentarily as the hail of fire offset its footing. Its armour, however, held up.

Mom should be happy with that, I guess.

Each bullet found its target and then promptly headed

off in a new direction as the armour deflected the missiles. Zaheera figured this would have been the case but hadn't expected the armour to be quite so impenetrable. She would need to be a lot more accurate.

Head and neck only.

Somebody groaned their final groan nearby as lead sank into flesh. Zaheera waited a moment and counted the various rifles firing. By her estimate there were more than ten guns firing. They still had a chance. The odds weren't entirely against them.

She unloaded the final few rounds in her magazine and then sprinted for the next building before hunkering down to reload. Alpha was only two buildings away. Without much need for cover, the bot's effectiveness was becoming quite apparent. The air filled with the cries of the dying. It was fast becoming a slaughter and Zaheera realised her earlier thought about favourable odds was about to be turned on its head.

The growl of a Land Rover sounded as a vehicle roared into camp. Zaheera, reloading her magazine, peered around from cover and saw the baby-faced Corporal Williams at the wheel with Steve, looking petrified, in the passenger seat, apparently unwillingly holding a gun. The Land Rover skidded to a halt, driver side facing the fight. The young corporal bounced out, rifle over his back and pistol in hand, and began unloading as he crab-walked to cover, yelling at Steve to do the same. Alpha was now surrounded on all sides.

Williams, you beautiful bastard!

Zaheera tossed her final grenade and popped out of cover as shrapnel once more went in search of flesh in which to bury itself. She held her breath and aimed steady.

One ... Two ...

A single shot rang out and hit the bot in the neck, putting it flat on its back. Jack and Baz appeared from cover seconds later, rifles aimed at the bot.

Zaheera saw its arm twitch at the last moment.

Oh, no.

Alpha, still gripping the assault rifle it had picked up, fired a short burst at both soldiers as they stepped over.

Prrrrap, prrrrap, and they were down.

They were dead before they knew it.

It got to its feet, shaken but by no means broken. Besides a few scratches to its armour, Zaheera wondered whether they had managed to damage it at all. *It's a fucking tank!*

It's a tank.

It's a tank ...

She'd fought tanks before. Tanks always had a weakness, usually at the back. The quickest way she'd seen tanks immobilised was either explosive force aimed at the rear or by disabling the caterpillar tracks.

Both options usually meant getting up close and sticking something nasty on the offending target. Firing endlessly from a distance was usually about as effective as a mosquito bite, irritating to the one being bitten, sure, but not much more.

No, she needed to get up close.

So be it.

She fired another burst and then switched to her left, heading up the flank towards the armoury. Passing the remaining gaps between buildings she saw bodies splayed out, giving themselves back to the earth. The carnage reminded her of the convoy in Afghanistan. Different, but the same. Bodies everywhere. People bleeding out. Most dead, whilst those who weren't wished death would hurry up. They craved its sweet release. She saw the agony writ upon their faces. One soldier croaked something at her as she came up to the armoury. He lay on his back looking up at her. He'd spat blood up onto his face. His chest had caved in where the bullets had torn away most of the bone. 'Please,' he said, trying desperately to pull a pistol from his belt so he could end his agony. His trembling hands denied him his final wish.

It didn't matter.

The Reaper came for him in good time.

Zaheera moved on. She rounded the corner of the armoury and saw two soldiers still standing. They'd been here when she first came to the camp. The northern one she recognised as Kev. His accent had been almost impossible to understand at first. Each word had to be processed slowly, thought over and analysed, before moving to the next. The woman with him she knew was Becky.

'Private,' she whispered, reading the single chevron insignia on Becky's shoulder.

Both soldiers turned to face her. Their eyes opened wide as they recognised her.

'Major Bhukari, you're alive,' Kev said.

'Damned straight, Sergeant.' She rushed up alongside them, taking cover behind the wall.

'Zaheera, is that you?' Alpha's robotic voice boomed across the yard.

Kev and Becky looked at her, the whites of their eyes betraying their feigned calm. She instructed Kev to go around and see if Steve and the corporal were still alive. She and Becky turned to the corner, Zaheera taking point. She gently rolled her head round the wall, just enough for one eye to see, before snapping back as a burst of bullets hit where her head had just been.

'There you are,' Alpha said. 'Why don't you come on out? We can end this quicker.'

'Eat shit.'

'Always so dramatic, Zaheera. Is that language really necessary?'

'My mother isn't going to let you get away with this.'

'I know,' it said. 'But she and I will work it out once I'm done with you and your little entourage here.'

The worst part of Zaheera's career had always been witnessing things go wrong in front of her eyes and always being unable to stop them. No matter how much you trained a soldier, no matter how well prepared everybody was, the heat of battle always added another dimension. Nothing ever went to plan. Zaheera heard the footsteps and knew instantly that she'd lost her stronghold.

From the other side of the building, Steve, presumably thinking the bot too occupied with Zaheera to notice, decided to make a bid for the Cappelli house. To his credit he made it to the other side of the street, just.

The bullets that penetrated his back pushed him the rest of the way. He slammed into the Cappelli house door with his full weight and flopped to the ground. Alpha put a few more rounds into his corpse just to be sure.

Zaheera heard movement in the house on the other side. Sounded like somebody was sneaking out the back.

Alpha heard it too and made a move towards the door.

Zaheera and Becky popped out from behind cover, as did the sergeant and corporal on the other side. They fired in unison. Zaheera didn't hear a thing over her screams. She felt the assault rifle kick as round after round burst forth in flame.

Alpha turned in one sweeping motion and fired.

Zaheera ducked.

Becky was too slow.

As was one of the two on the other side of the building. It sounded like the corporal. It was always the youngest.

She checked her magazine. Empty. That was it, she was out. She sat against the wall, defeated, staring at Becky's body strewn across the ground.

A click sounded on the street. Alpha was out, too.

'Enough of these games,' it said. 'I have a date with your mother.' Alpha walked past the last building and pulled a wounded Kev to his feet. The sergeant managed a gurgled groan but didn't put up a fight. Alpha forced him into the driver's side of the Land Rover currently blocking the road, which Corporal Williams had so bravely driven up in, and got into the back seat holding a pistol to Kev's head, which it had liberated from his side.

'Drive,' she heard the bot yell.

Tyres bit through the mud as the engine roared.

The two were gone before Zaheera had got to her feet. She ran to the other side of the street and beat down the door. 'Susie!'

Susie was in the back, holding a mobile phone.

'Susie, we need to call my mother, now. Alpha's going after her.'

'Calling her now,' Susie said, handing the phone to her. 'Started ringing just after Alpha left.'

16

Ameera stared at her phoned as it buzzed furiously on her desk. Tiaan and Weronika looked to her.

'Are you going to get that?' Tiaan asked.

Ameera went to pick it up and then hesitated again. After all this radio silence, the pictures she'd seen of the destroyed bots from the drone footage, it couldn't be good news. Whatever Susie was calling to tell her, it wasn't going to be positive. *Please let Zaheera be alive.* After all these years trying to keep her safe, moving to America, losing Akeem, then losing Zaheera to the military lifestyle, she couldn't handle her worst nightmare becoming reality. It would be too cruel. This whole programme, her pursuit of technology that could protect and eventually replace soldiers, was all for her, so that one day she might not need to set foot on a battlefield again. The irony of her own design being the cause of her daughter's current life-threatening reality was not lost on her.

She picked the phone up and answered. 'Hello?'

'Mom?'

Alhamdulillah.

'Zaheera?'

'It's me, Mom.'

'I'm so glad you're okay. Please, tell me you're okay.' Ameera heard her daughter weeping on the other end of the phone and let forth her own stream of tears. She could hold them back no longer. Her daughter was alive. That was all she had wanted to know. The pressure release from within almost caused her to pass out. She sat down in her chair and exhaled.

'I'm okay, Mom. I'm alive. But something's gone wrong.'

'I know, I know,' Ameera said. 'When we lost contact we sent a drone over the training area. I saw the dismembered bots scattered on the hillside. I saw the bodies in camp. For a moment, I thought ... I thought ...'

'It's okay,' Zaheera said. 'I'm really okay, I promise. But you're in danger, Mom. Alpha, it's gone rogue. All of this ... I don't know what got into it.'

'It doesn't matter now.'

'It does,' her daughter pleaded. 'It said it was coming for you. You need to get out of there. You need to get out of there *now*, Mom.'

Ameera leaned back in her chair, a smile creeping across her face. 'Do you remember what your father used to say about responsibility?'

A pause on the other end of the line. 'He said that in order to have any impact on the world, first we must take responsibility.'

'Yes. This is my mess, Zaheera. I will deal with it accordingly.'

The tears became full-blown sobs on the other end. 'I'm coming, Mom. I'm coming for you.'

Ameera wiped the tears from her eyes. 'I love you, Zaheera. I have always loved you, you know that, but what you have perhaps never known is how proud of you I am. I didn't want to encourage your choice of career. It was too painful to watch. But I am proud of you. You have been the highlight of my life.' She paused momentarily and took a deep a deep breath. 'I'm sorry for dragging you into this. I did it for you. I thought I was helping.'

'You just hold on,' her daughter said. 'I'm going to alert everybody about Alpha's intentions. By the time it gets to London, the entire armed forces are going to be waiting.'

'No,' Ameera said. 'Too many have died already. I need to take care of this. Nobody else can shut this thing down. Don't put anybody else at risk. Promise me.'

'Fine,' Zaheera said eventually. 'I'm on my way.'

'I love you, Zaheera.'

'I love you, too, Mom.'

Ameera ended the call and placed her phone back down on her desk. Tiaan and Weronika were still standing in the room. Both looked like they too had not entirely been able to prevent the tears from flowing. Ameera smiled at them. 'You need to go. Be with your families. I don't want you to be here for what happens next.'

Tiaan had that same indecipherable expression on his face. She couldn't tell if he was angry or confused. *Probably a little of both.*

'I don't have any family in this country, boss,' he said. 'I think I'll stay.'

'Tiaan, I'm not kidding. You saw the drone footage. This isn't going to end with everybody skipping out the gate and down the yellow brick road, hand in hand.'

'If it's all the same, I'll be staying.'

Ameera stifled a laugh. 'You're a stubborn prick, you know that?'

'*Ja*, I've heard that before.' He returned her smile.

'I'll be staying, too,' Weronika said. 'No point letting you two have all the fun.'

'No,' Ameera said. 'Don't be ridiculous. You don't need to do this.'

'Yes, I do,' Weronika said. 'To effect change, first we must take responsibility, right?'

'Something like that, yes.'

'Besides, you lot wouldn't know how to work a thing in this building without me here to help.'

'She has a point,' Tiaan said.

'Okay,' Ameera said. 'We need to evacuate the building without causing alarm. Get everybody out safely. We have a few hours before Alpha gets here. I need to prepare.'

It took a couple of hours to empty the building but eventually they succeeded. The only people left at the Cappelli Technologies building were herself, Tiaan, Weronika and the young security guard on duty. Ameera recognised him. Martin. Or something like that. A big, burly lad with a fierce ginger beard. It added years to him. Made the youngster look quite intimidating, too, if his size didn't do that for you first. Ameera liked him. The West Country boy was always so chipper. He'd lost some of that chipperness, though, when she'd explained the situation to him. 'I don't want you getting involved, Martin. I just need you to lock the building down once Alpha is in and then get as far away from here as you can.'

'Yes, ma'am.' His furrowed brow betrayed an internal

battle to push the matter further but his exterior control eventually won over. He said no more.

'And if my daughter arrives, don't let her in. You take her with you, away from here and you protect her. I don't want anybody else entering the building once Alpha is in. You got it?'

'I do,' he said.

'Good. Thank you, Martin. Send a message to my office when you see Alpha on the premises.'

'Will do.' He gave her a curt nod and turned his attention back to the bank of security screens he had been monitoring when Ameera had stepped into his office near reception.

Ameera took the lift back to her now empty floor and walked to her office. She made herself a tea and sat back in her chair. Shutting Alpha down would be damned near impossible, she knew that. Weronika, apparently having similar concerns, knocked on her door shortly after.

'Is this a bad time?'

'All things considered? No. What's on your mind?' Ameera asked.

'Well, I was checking the data on each bot and there's so much missing.'

'Considering they got cut from the cloud, yeah, that makes sense.'

'Sure, but Alpha's data trail is patchy well before that.'

'What do you mean?'

'Alpha doesn't have the same telemetry tracking as the others did. But, like, from the beginning. It's not so much that the data is missing. I don't think it was ever there. From the moment Alpha left this office, it had complete autonomy, even from us.'

'Is this the part where you accuse me of something?'

'I was hoping we'd cut the shit and you could just admit what you were doing.'

'That's why I like you, Weronika: straight to the point, without fail. Others might find you intimidating, but for me, I always know where I stand with you. You've always been my litmus test.'

'Thanks, I guess.'

'You're right, Alpha is different. He was my first.'

'He?'

'I gave him a male voice, didn't I?'

'You gave them *all* male voices. I thought that was for the same reason we didn't give them all the silicone skins we designed, or facial features. Wasn't it all about simplicity? Just something that could point and shoot better than a human soldier?'

'Yes and no. Alpha was my first, though. That made him special. I never had a second kid so I don't know if parents get the same feeling the second time round, but I didn't get the same feeling with the other bots. Alpha was unique. I wanted to call him Adam. Even told him that once. Said I thought it was funny. He said he liked it, but we agreed to stick to Alpha. We decided to keep everything uniform so nobody would notice.'

'What do you mean "we decided"? Were you two conspiring together?'

'Conspiring? No. *Learning.* I gave the other bots all the same tech. They had the same artificial intelligence encoded into them and each one learned things in slightly different ways based on whatever patterns they witnessed. None of them evolved like Alpha, though. He was so smart. His intellect was off the charts, before I'd even given him a body. When he was just code that could talk. You should have seen it. He understood subtlety and nuance. Picked things up faster than any human I've seen. Developed his own character. Weronika, he developed emotions. The others all made observations. At a stretch, we might say they had certain characteristics that could be interpreted as similar to having a personality, but with Alpha there was no question.'

'Why?'

'Why, what?' Ameera asked.

'Why would you take such a risk on a piece of code?'

'He's more than just code,' she said defensively. She sipped her tea and looked at Weronika, whose expression sat somewhere between confusion and anger. 'Careful,' Ameera said. 'Tiaan walks around with that same expression most of the time. You don't want to be confused for that oaf, do you?'

'I'm trying to understand why you would let something so advanced run so free, regardless of what you were learning.'

'You're not seeing the big picture. The volume of data, the sheer scale of it, was unimaginable. I learned more spending a day with Alpha than I did in six months with the other bots. It was because of him that I was able to advance the tech this much.'

'Congratulations, you created a monster.'

'I know that, *now*,' Ameera said. 'The truth is we wouldn't have come this far this quickly without me doing so, and time wasn't on my side. My daughter had already done one tour of Afghanistan. Every day she was out there getting guns pointed at her increased the odds of something going wrong. I was so relieved to find out that she'd survived her first tour relatively unscathed.' Ameera ran a hand through her hair, fixating on one strand that kept falling back into her eye. 'It never ends with the military, though. I knew there would be another tour soon enough. The programme had to be accelerated. Every day we delayed was another day my daughter was in danger, another day her life was at risk.'

'So you put all our careers, not to mention the lives of all the soldiers involved, including your daughter's, at risk?'

'I did what I had to do. Any parent would do the same.'

'It wasn't your decision to make.'

Ameera met Weronika's accusatory stare. 'Are you a mother, Weronika?'

'You know I'm not.'

'Right, so don't talk about something you cannot comprehend. You have no idea what it's like watching every news report, day in, day out, reading every newspaper article mentioning the war, waiting to see your worst fears confirmed. It never lets up. You sit there, scanning *everything*, rejoicing a little and hating yourself for it when you hear it's someone else's child that has been taken. Eventually that got to me, too. I wanted it *all* to stop. Imagine all those mothers, fathers, brothers, sisters, sitting at home, waiting to hear if the one they love wasn't going to be coming home. I was uniquely positioned to help end it all. And so you're damned right I pushed it as far as I could. I risked it all to see this programme through. If I have played a part, however small, in realising a world in which we no longer need to send our boys and girls off to battle so that those in suits can better manipulate the world's markets to their own advantage, then I'll die a happy woman.'

'Well, you probably are going to die for it, so congratulations on that. I'm not sure anything from this programme will be pushed forward when they find our bodies tomorrow. I fear that if anything, you have stalled the progress of that which you seek.'

'You misunderstand humanity,' Ameera said. 'It is an

unstoppable plague sometimes. Once set in motion, it will pursue something until its very end. I knew that. I *know* that. So I stepped in to course correct. You're right, whatever happens here today may well cause concern amongst a few, but not those who are financially invested. Not those with actual decision-making power. And really, it's only those who need to be convinced. They will pursue this because they've already seen what they stand to gain. The powerless will find something else to be angry about next week. It may not happen exactly as I planned, but this idea will become a reality. If the price is my life, so be it.'

Weronika hesitated a moment. 'Fair enough.'

Whatever Ameera had said, it appeared to have struck a chord.

'It's not easy being the first one through the door, Weronika. There is no reward for this. There is only a price: responsibility. I only want to help progress humanity to its next logical evolution.'

'Sure.'

It seemed Weronika was finally on board, or at least no longer as critical. Either way, Ameera was taking that as a win. 'Okay then. Now, let's figure out how we're going to deal with Alpha when he gets here.'

THEY WORKED on for another couple of hours, preparing for the worst. Ameera knew that Alpha was coming for her specifically. That would be the bot's primary concern. She was, after all, the one who had designed it all. Everybody else involved at Cappelli Technologies only knew pieces of the puzzle. Ameera was the crucial knowledge holder. With her out of the way, Alpha would be able to do as he pleased. She was the final hurdle.

'If Alpha isn't connected to the cloud and is running remotely, we at least know its hard drives will be nearly maxed out by now,' Weronika said. 'It'll be using everything it's got just to maintain functionality. I say we DDoS it. We've still got plenty of data in the system from previous security tests. We can lump it all together and create the biggest DDoS attack yet. It won't be able to withstand the barrage of traffic from a denial-of-service attack.'

'You know we designed its security to withstand that,' Ameera said.

'Yes, but with it no longer connected to the cloud, it won't be able to patch in updates, so an updated attack based on a flaw in the version of its operating system might work.'

'It's a long shot,' Ameera said.

'Got any better ideas?'

'Not right now, no.'

'In that case, I'll get on it.'

'You do that,' Ameera said. She didn't have the heart to tell Weronika that Alpha's unrestrained AI was likely to have developed its own security updates by now. Alpha had most likely updated most aspects of its operating system remotely in order to prevent exactly this kind of situation from playing out. The mere fact that nobody had been able to secure any connection to the bots when they all went offline told her that whatever Alpha was up to, it had been thought through already. They were still trying to get off the blocks whilst Alpha was cruising through the finish line. All they could do was try to lock him in the building and conduct some kind of physical attack. If he could be restrained, Ameera knew she could remove his hard drives, reset his system, or do whatever the hell she pleased. Restraining him wasn't exactly going to be an easy task, though. He would know by now that she was aware of the situation. They were two sharks, circling each other, waiting for one to make an error so the other could swoop in and deal the killing bite.

The direct line on Ameera's desk broke her train of thought. It was an internal number. 'Yes, Martin?'

'Something's pulling up on me screens, ma'am.'

'What is it?'

'Looks like an old military Land Rover. Some poor betwaddled mucker's in the driving seat. I can't see yer mate, though.'

'Can you patch the feed through to my office, Martin?'

'Sure can, one sec.'

Ameera's screen filled with a fuzzy night camera view. A dark, presumably green, but hard to tell in the light, Land Rover pulled up to the entrance. The driver lifted his hands off the wheel in surrender.

It's like he has a gun to his head.

She was right. A second later the man's head burst forward, the contents of his skull blasted all over the windscreen. He'd been shot from behind.

The Land Rover's rear driver's-side door opened and out stepped Alpha into the night, holding a pistol in its hand.

Ameera called through to Tiaan. 'He's here. Make sure you and Weronika stay out of the way until absolutely necessary. Let him come to me. That's what he wants.' After he'd confirmed they were ready she called Martin back and asked him to leave the minute Alpha was through the doors and locked in.

Then she waited, watching on the security feed as Alpha made it into the building, passing reception, into one of the lifts. Butterflies took wing in her stomach as she shifted in her seat. *Keep calm.* She heard the ping of the lift on her floor and saw him step out and walk over to her. He looked like he'd been in the wars. His armour was disfigured from gunshot damage and mud caked most of his shell.

'Hello, Ameera. It's good to see you.'

'Hello, Alpha.'

17

Z aheera surveyed the carnage that was the Brecon Training Camp. Bodies were strewn all down the main street. Steve's corpse lay at the front of the Cappelli house door, its back riddled with lead. In reality the skirmish had probably only lasted a matter of minutes but to Zaheera it had felt like a lifetime. She was worn out. The effect from the adrenaline needle that Shannon had jammed into her leg in the back of the Land Rover as they'd driven to camp had mostly worn off. Pain had returned to every part of her body.

She exited the Cappelli house and stepped out onto the street. Corporal Williams's corpse could be seen on the other side, as could Becky's, round the far side of the building where the corporal lay. The air was filled with a hot, wet stench. Zaheera's battlefield experience consisted of warmer climates where bodies were normally covered quickly in flies and other undesirables. In the cold, drenched Welsh countryside the bodies seemed almost pathetic. The clouds opened and rain started to wash the blood into the gutters, cleansing the battlefield. To her the bodies looked more sinister all washed and blood-free. The blood ran down the street in a maroon stream, like paint being washed from a building site.

She liberated a couple of bodies of their assault rifles and ammo and was walking down the street as Susie and Shannon stepped out of the Cappelli house after her.

'Where are you going?' Susie asked.

'London,' Zaheera said as she walked up to the black van the bots had originally arrived in.

'We're coming with you,' Shannon said.

'No, you're not.'

'With all due respect,' Shannon said, 'you've seen what that thing is capable of. If you're going after it, you're going to need assistance.'

'Yeah,' Susie agreed with Shannon. 'I might not be able to shoot like Shannon can, but I can help in other ways.'

'That so?'

'That's so. I'm the only one here who knows how to operate Cappelli tech. Guns don't seem to have had the desired effect, if you hadn't already noticed. My guess is that it's going to have to be something a little more technical than brute force that brings that thing down.'

She had a point. Zaheera had done her best to bring Alpha down but nothing had worked. Not guns, not grenades, and certainly not hand-to-hand combat. Her mother really had built a force to be reckoned with. If you ignored the rogue murderous mentality it had developed, it really was a fine soldier. She hesitated as she opened the driver's-side door. It wasn't a matter of pride anymore. She didn't want to involve anybody else who wasn't absolutely necessary but she realised her plan to save her mother pretty much consisted of the approach Susie had just deemed ineffective. 'All right,' she said. 'Get in.'

SHANNON SPENT most of the drive patching them up.

'I'm fine,' Zaheera pleaded as Shannon continued to fuss over her while she drove. 'You want me to get us pulled over for driving one-handed?'

'You still have cuts all over,' Shannon warned.

'And they'll still be there if we make it through the night. You can deal with them then.'

'Suit yourself,' Shannon said.

'Thank you. Just hit me with one of those needles again when we get near and I'll be fine.'

'It's your funeral,' she said, before turning her attention to Susie.

Zaheera kept her eyes on the road for hours. It was a long, silent drive, despite Shannon's medical assistance, as each person contemplated what they were driving into. Her forearm muscles tensed, gripping the wheel tightly as she turned off the motorway and started the final stretch through the outskirts of London. This was it. No turning back now.

'You think we stand a chance?' Shannon asked.

'As good a chance as any,' Zaheera said, unsure of whether she was trying to convince herself or the others.

'If this were Afghanistan and you'd just lost the same amount of people, would you still push on or would you retreat?'

'I lost a lot of people in Afghanistan. And we did push on.'

'Did you win?'

'I survived.'

Shannon appeared unconvinced with Zaheera's answer.

'We can do it,' Susie said. 'The Cappelli building is one

of the most advanced buildings around. We can use it to our advantage.'

'How so?' Shannon asked.

'You know, like close off certain sections at a time. Guide Alpha where we need it to go. We can be more strategic with our attack.'

'You know to operate all that tech?'

'Sure I do. Had a hand in designing some of it, in fact. We just gotta hope Alpha's still in there when we arrive, hope Ameera holds out long enough to give us a chance.' She looked up into the rear-view mirror and caught Zaheera's gaze. 'Sorry.'

'Don't worry. My mother will hold out. She's tough as nails, that one.'

'Runs in the family,' Shannon said.

Zaheera had no answer to that. The truth was she didn't have her mother's strength. Her mother had never broken down after her husband's death. Sure, she'd eventually moved to a new country, but that was more of a blank-page-type thing. She'd persevered through the agony and come out the other side stronger, more determined. Hell, she came out with a mission. Zaheera, on the other hand, had crumbled, unsure of what to do with herself or where to go. By her mother's standards, she was an embarrassment. Her mother hadn't required rehabilitation at some Harley Manor equivalent like she had. No, she was nowhere near as tough as her mother.

THE STREETS of South London passed by in a flash as Zaheera drove through the dark, driving almost on autopilot. Had she not been driving stick-shift, she might well have nodded off. Stick kept her focus, thankfully. Streetlights zipped by overhead in a saffron blur. At one point she almost missed their turning. Susie, somewhat more familiar with the route, called her on it as she almost took a turn heading north towards the river. Just in time.

Eventually the Cappelli Technologies building came into sight. Zaheera eased her foot off the gas and slowed to a crawl.

'How's it look?' Susie asked, leaning forward through the middle gap, her head appearing adjacent to Zaheera's.

'Looks fine to me. Pretty normal. Anything look out of the ordinary to you?'

Susie looked long and hard, squinting her eyes like she was looking for some far-off animal on safari. 'Nope,' she said after a while. 'Nothing out of the ordinary that jumps out to me.'

'It always this quiet?'

'This time of day, yeah.'

'Well,' Zaheera said. 'At least there aren't any bodies lining the street.'

'You got that right,' Shannon said. 'What are the chances your mother's sorted it all already and we're free and clear?'

'About as good as my chances of not having nightmares after all this.'

'Greeeeat.'

Parked just to the side of the entrance was the green Land Rover that Alpha had commandeered when it took Kev hostage as its driver. The sergeant's blood could be seen splattered across the inside of the windscreen.

Susie gasped when she saw the sergeant keeled over the steering wheel. Zaheera could hear her stifled sobs and was grateful that the darkness hid what was likely a gruesome sight.

'Fucking bastard,' Shannon muttered under her breath.

'Save it,' Zaheera said. 'Channel it, and when you do run into that piece of shit collection of bolts and screws, you show it exactly how you feel.'

'I'll show it, all right,' Shannon said. 'You're all going to have to get in line.'

'As long as that thing dies by the time we're through, I couldn't give a flying fuck who pulls the trigger,' Zaheera said. She coasted the van into the car park and came to a stop well before the entrance. She had expected to feel trepidation or some form of anxiety, but instead she felt the same tingling anticipation that she had felt as a soldier on tour before heading out on patrol. Knowing you were heading into guaranteed contact had a way of ratcheting up the nerves somewhat. After too long trying to avoid it, trying to change the course of her existence away from combat, to duck it all, she realised this was what she wanted, what she needed. Her body came alive in moments like these. It was alive now, heart pounding, vision and hearing heightened, she was in the zone. The rest of the world was blocked out. All there was now was her, her squad, and whomever was in the building right in front of her. Alpha was somewhere in there, she could feel it. Maybe it was watching, maybe they would have the element of surprise. It didn't matter to Zaheera now. She was here, ready to fight, *wanting* to fight, and that, in and of itself, was something. Vindication of her career choice, perhaps. She knew who she was and didn't need to explain it to anybody. Her mother may not like it but she didn't have to. Zaheera just needed to become who she chose to be. She wished she were back at Harley Manor for a moment so she could explain to Doctor Griffiths that she had finally realised what she was and what that meant to her. He would no doubt be happy for her.

Behind her, Shannon pulled out the weapons they had

lifted from the corpses back at the Brecon Training Camp and handed them out. Susie was given a pistol – emergency only, of course – while Zaheera received an assault rifle, multiple magazines of spare ammo, grenades, and a couple of pistols, also with spare magazines. She thought again about whether or not they should be calling for backup but decided her mother had been right. It only risked more people dying. They were going to need to sort this on their own.

'Everybody ready?'

Both Shannon and Susie had gone silent, entering their own zones. They nodded.

'All right. Move out.'

THEY CREPT SILENTLY UP to the entrance. Inside the lights were still on but Zaheera couldn't see anybody moving about. She pushed her assault rifle behind her back and gently eased the door open, half expecting it to have been locked.

So far, so good.

All three of them entered, moving quietly and crouching low, sticking to the walls. The door clicked behind them. A metallic hammer sounded as the locking mechanism shut off their means of escape.

Zaheera backtracked and tested the door again. She figured somebody had been watching them and had locked them in.

No way out.

The other two acknowledged her signal. They moved over to reception. Nobody was there, so Susie took control of the computer. Seconds later they each had access cards to the whole building. They would be able to move freely throughout.

'Yer mam said I shouldn't be letting you in,' a gruff voice whispered behind them.

Zaheera spun, rifle at the ready, and found herself aiming at the chest of a burly young man with a big ginger beard.

He smiled at her. 'You must be Zaheera. All right there, Suse?' he asked, looking over Zaheera's shoulder.

'Hey, Martin,' Susie said. 'It's cool, Zaheera. Martin's the guard here. He's on our side.'

Zaheera lowered her weapon as Susie got up from the desk at reception and hugged Martin.

'Is it here?'

'You mean that metal tosspot? Yeah, it's 'ere all right. Jammed all the camera feeds when it rolled up, mind. I been hunkered down in me security office ever since. Ameera said to stay outta the way and make sure Zaheera here never entered the building. Bugger that, I say. She's gonna need a bloomin' army to take that thing down, I reckon. I set the building to lock itself down after you entered, so unless you all got plans to be jumpin' outta windows, we're stuck in here for now. Don't want our metal friend to be walkin' out the door all on his larry, you see. I was hoping you lot wouldn't be far behind. As soon as yer mam said you were on yer way, I knew you'd be coming with weapons. Not much I could do 'ere with this except swat flies,' he said, holding a collapsible metal rod. 'Or tickle me arse. But that's about it.'

'You've done well, Martin,' Susie said.

'Well, let's save all the self-congratulatory nonsense for later,' he said. 'I'm worried about Ameera.'

'Let's get moving, then,' Zaheera said. She handed him

one of her pistols and a spare magazine. 'You ever used one of these?'

'I had a cousin when I was a kid. He was always finding weapons for us to mess around with. We used to head out on our bikes into the fields and set up targets with old loo rolls. Then we'd spend the day drinkin', smokin', and shootin' with whatever weapon he'd found. Once or twice he brought us a pistol. I'm not gonna promise yer I'm a better shot than you, what with all yer fancy training. But I got more loo rolls than my cousin ever did.'

'Sounds like you should have joined the military,' Shannon said. 'Most boys with a gun fetish do.'

'Nah,' he said. 'Firstly, it wasn't no gun fetish, it was more of a hobby. Secondly, it'd get in the way of my other two favourite hobbies.' He caressed his belly with pride. 'Cider might put hairs on yer chest an' all, but it don't half slow you down. Add a bit of smoke to that and you can be damned sure I ain't got no hope of ever keepin' up with them skinny runts runnin' around all yessirin' and nosirrin'. Besides,' he winked at Susie, 'I'm too pretty to be kept all cooped up in a barracks somewhere.'

Susie smiled for the first time since Zaheera had met her. Martin, it seemed, was pretty good company. She closed Martin's hand around the pistol with her own. 'I hope you're as sharp as you are funny, Martin.'

'I guess we'll find out soon enough,' he said, the smile on his face withdrawing behind the safety of his beard. 'Come on. Ameera's office is this way.'

The four of them moved quietly to the staircase, the squeak of rubber-soled shoes providing the only audio to their otherwise stealthy approach. Martin informed them that the lifts had been disabled by Alpha. He'd apparently tried to follow the bot up to Ameera's floor but decided against it after coming up against the disabled lift. It had made him think twice, eventually deciding it might be best to wait until Zaheera and any weapons arrived. The staircase operated on its own security system, according to Martin, being a fire exit and all, and therefore wasn't locked down when Alpha disabled the lifts. They made their way up to Ameera's floor.

'You sure you wanna do this?' Martin asked Zaheera.

'I'm sure.'

Martin gently loosed the door handle.

Zaheera and Shannon went through first, each at an angle, covering the opposite section of the floor.

'Clear,' Zaheera said.

'Clear,' came Shannon's reply.

Zaheera kept her eye trained down the barrel's sights. The floor had multiple rooms, and seemed to lead down a hallway to a large open-plan floor at the other end of the staircase. They would have to check every room, despite her instinct telling her they wouldn't find anything. This wasn't a time for a lackadaisical approach. There could be no errors.

The first room was just some kind of IT room, with servers stacked throughout, bleeping lights going off on each one and a fan somewhere in there working on overdrive. It sounded like a small plane about to take off. Zaheera checked for anyone hiding behind the server stacks but found none.

She moved onto the next room.

Some kind of meeting room. Empty. She moved on. The others trailed just behind her.

It was only when they got to the open-plan part of the floor that Zaheera's anxiety ratcheted up a few more notches. This was too quiet. They should have heard something by now, or seen something. The eerie silence was doing nothing to calm her nerves. She recalled her first visit to this building. This had been the floor on which her mother had introduced her to Alpha. The bot had been standing docile in the middle of the floor before waking up as they came near. Zaheera had half expected to walk into the same scene this time round. But no, no Alpha in the middle of the floor. Just endless pods of desks, filled with screens and keyboards, completely interchangeable with any other office anywhere in the world. Stale, uninviting, prison-like. If ever someone asked why Zaheera had chosen a military career and not a corporate one, she'd instantly start describing the lifeless, soul-sucking insignificance that was an office. This one was no different.

Her stomach gurgled with anticipation. The frustration of not seeing or hearing anything sent her mind into overdrive, exploring all the possibilities.

In the end there was only one.

Zaheera saw it as she walked up the pods towards her mother's office. The door was ajar and there, face down on her desk in a pool of her own blood was her mother.

She was too late.

SHANNON TRIED to grab her shoulder but Zaheera had already forgotten all semblance of control. She whipped the assault rifle behind her back and ran into her mother's office, not checking her surroundings, not caring one iota for her own safety. She propped her mother's body up in the chair to scan for the wound. Her throat had been cut from side to side, leaving her head lolled forward as dark maroon, almost chestnut-brown blood spilled forward down her front. Zaheera knew she didn't need to check for a pulse but she checked anyway.

Nothing.

And then, without warning, the tears came. She hugged her mother's body, not caring about the blood that was getting all over her.

THE OTHERS KEPT watch outside the room as Zaheera wailed uncontrollably.

'We were too slow,' Shannon cursed quietly.

'I can't believe it,' Susie said, wiping the tears from her eyes. 'Alpha actually did it.'

'You better believe it,' Shannon said. 'And we're still locked in the building *with* it.'

18

Zaheera wiped the blood from her mother's face and neck, sobbing quietly all the while. Martin, Shannon and Susie all remained outside the room, letting her have her moment. Zaheera couldn't believe it. All her effort to make it in time. For nothing. No matter what she tried, everybody around her died. It was some kind of sick joke. First her father, taken well before his time, then her fellow soldiers, one by one journeying to the other side, leaving her stranded upon her own shore, all alone. The one person she'd always known was there, somewhere in the background, like a safety blanket you could return to in times of need, was now gone, too. Despite having always felt it, she was, for the first time in her life, truly alone. There was no one left.

She clung to her mother's cooling body, desperate to somehow convey to the lifeless corpse how much she had meant to her, regardless of what she might have said to the contrary at various points over the last few years. It was, of course, no use. 'I'm sorry,' she whispered into her mother's ear. 'I'm so sorry.'

The ridiculousness of talking to a corpse was not lost on her but she didn't care. She needed to say it, even if the intended recipient was deaf to her proclamations of regret. This was her penance for not having said it sooner, when she could have, when her mother might have heard.

As she had with her father, she wished that they had had more time. Wished she had spent that time telling her mother how much she had meant to her. Or at least just spent that time together, making memories with each other, instead of spending it worlds apart, each too stubborn to tell the other how much they needed one another. Each one unable to get over the death of Zaheera's father, unable to mourn together. The terrible event that should have brought them closer together in fact drove them apart.

Instead they had found their own ways to mourn. Both had thrown themselves at their work like it was some sort of divine purpose. *Maybe it was.* They had both been successful in their own right. Yet success never filled the hole left behind. At least for Zaheera – the more she had thrown herself into her military career, the more she missed her father, and the harder it got to walk into each new day without him. Zaheera's life felt to her like a long and ancient journey trudging through a desert, one in which her father had fallen and lay behind her somewhere on her path, and each new day she awoke further along the path, further from him, whether she wanted to be or not. Time healed nothing. It only blurred her vision when she looked back over her shoulder. Sometimes she saw a mirage, some old memory highlighting better days, but it was never real. Memories were selective. They only included the good stuff. Death had a funny way of erasing the truth behind history. In the end it was almost impossible to recall events as they had actually happened. They became memories of memories. Refined to such a point as to be merely anecdotes, cheap thrills that brought back the occasional smile.

Then there were the times she looked back over her shoulder at the path she had walked through life and saw only monsters. They lay in wait, taking her by surprise like wolves hunting in the night, feeding on fear and indecision, turning doubt into crippling insecurity. It became easier not to look back. Instead she trained herself to keep her eyes only on the path ahead. Plough forward at all costs. Never engage the past. What was there but misery and loss? Ahead lay the unknown, but unknown danger was better than known horror.

And so she chose the former.

That, in and of itself, felt momentous for Zaheera. It was at the very least a choice, *her* choice. It was a decision to do something. Not to wallow in insecurity. Whatever the dangers in the path ahead, it was better than letting the monsters win.

She unclipped the blood-covered gold necklace from her mother's neck and placed it in her shirt pocket before buttoning it up. Why she wanted a memento she did not know. Despite her compulsion to grieve over the loss of others, she did not consider herself sentimental. She didn't keep *things*, she kept memories, but lacking many of those she and her mother shared, perhaps a memento on this occasion would suffice. It helped, at least a little, to have something physical of her mother's near to her heart.

Shannon knocked gently on the door. She entered the room and shuffled her feet, clearly not wanting to force Zaheera to leave her mother. She cleared her throat before looking at her feet.

'It's okay,' Zaheera said. 'I know. We need to move.'

'When you're ready,' Shannon said.

'I'm ready.' She wiped a few strands of loose hair from her mother's face and kissed her forehead. 'I hope he's waiting for you on the other side. Give him a kiss from me.'

'ZAHEERA,' Martin said, looking for the right words. 'We're all … we're sorry.'

'It's okay,' Zaheera said, wiping her bloodied hands on her shirt. 'She knew what she was getting into. This was the risk.'

'Speaking of the risk,' Susie said, 'I think Alpha's still in the building.'

'Makes sense. You didn't see it exit, Martin?'

'Me? No. B'sides, you lot arrived not long after it. If it had left the building, you'd probably have run smack bang into it coming down the street. No, it's in here somewhere, waiting for us.'

'Right you are, Martin. Right you are.'

All four of them spun round at the sound of the robotic voice.

19

'I guess that saves us wonderin' where you were hidin',' Martin said. He kicked over the table in front of him and sent computer screens and keyboards hurtling through the office air before clattering to the ground.

Shannon took Martin's lead and did the same with the desk in front of her.

Susie, untrained in the art of quick physical reactions, had barely moved before she was sent flying by the bullets that sprang forth from Alpha's assault rifle. She hit the wall of Ameera's office with a thud and flopped to the ground.

Zaheera, somewhat stunned by Alpha's presence, was brought back to reality as Susie's body lay just outside the door in front of her. 'You!' she yelled, looking dead ahead at the bot.

'Yes, *me*,' the bot replied in a sinister drawl.

She pulled her assault rifle from her back and squeezed the trigger. It burst into life in a cacophony of pops, echoing round the room like popcorn in a bowl.

Her aim was better than it had been back in Brecon Training Camp. No more spray and pray. As she had learned then, she aimed for the bot's head, and heard the satisfying *ting, ting, ting,* as the shots found their mark. She saw Alpha stagger back as the flurry of fire proved momentarily insurmountable, even for the battle-ready machine.

Alpha fired from the hip whilst taking a few steps back, and then took cover behind a corridor wall towards the back of the room.

Shannon, still taking cover behind one of the overturned office tables, let out a howl and then dropped to ground, gurgling as the blood filling her mouth threatened to choke her. The ineffective table had been reduced mostly to sawdust.

Martin reached over from his cover point and dragged Shannon's body back into Ameera's office. Zaheera laid down cover fire for a moment, before then doing the same with Susie's. She looked into Susie's eyes as she propped her into a sitting position against the wall, near to where Martin had placed Shannon. Susie, whilst clearly on the edge, was still alive. Just. Her pupils were dilated and she drooled as she tried to mumble something.

'Shhh,' Zaheera said. 'It doesn't matter. You're safe behind this wall.'

Zaheera thought of how many times she'd lied to wounded soldiers in battles before. How many times she'd said that backup was on its way, or how close the evac chopper was, if they could just hold on. The lies, she realised, were not always for the wounded. Sometimes they worked just as well for the liar, giving false hope, setting the mind to a more positive outcome. It had a tremendous placebo effect, drawing strength from some unknown well deep within. Often backup did eventually follow, and evac choppers did arrive, and every time she had survived. In the meantime, she had been able to carry on. There might not be any backup on this occasion but at least they were in cover for now.

'Martin, the door,' she said. 'I'll patch them up, you keep that metal prick pinned back. Aim for the head. It doesn't like it.'

'Right you are.' He placed a hand on Shannon's shoulder. 'Hold on, love. This'll all be over in a minute and we can get you outta here.'

Shannon grinned a maroon-toothed smile back at him and then flopped her head forward, its weight proving too heavy to hold up.

Zaheera investigated the bullet wounds on Susie's body as Martin left Shannon and fired short, sharp bursts from cover. Susie had been hit twice in the arm and once on the side of her rib cage. Splinters of bone were visible in the blood that oozed out with every breath. 'It's not that bad,' Zaheera said, again wondering if she were embellishing the truth at all. 'They all went straight through. I can patch them up and have you right as rain in no time.'

'Grmmnt,' came the gargled reply.

She removed a bandage and duct tape from her bag and wrapped it around Susie's wounded arm and ribcage, which Susie didn't show any appreciation for in the moment. 'This stuff is magic,' she said, biting off a strip of tape. 'It'll keep you in one piece, all right.' Without warning Susie, she pulled out an adrenaline needle, too, and jammed it into Susie's thigh. 'You can thank me later. Trust me, this is the good shit.'

Having patched Susie back up as best she could, Zaheera moved over to check on Shannon. Her still frame and drooped head sent a shiver down Zaheera's neck. She checked for a pulse.

Nothing.

She tilted Shannon's head back and forced an eye open. Nothing.

She was gone.

No matter what she did, people kept dying on her.

'I'm sorry,' she whispered to the second corpse currently occupying the room. 'How we looking, Martin?' she asked, turning her attention once more to the problem at hand. A few shots hit the wall just above Martin's head, kicking up a small cloud of dust.

He ducked back into cover. 'Oh, great,' he said. 'We're havin' a right old time, the friendly bastard and me.'

'Glad to hear it,' she said. She propped herself up against the near-side wall of the door and laid down a few rounds of suppressing fire.

Martin balled his hand into a fist signalling her to stop. They waited with bated breath for a moment.

No response.

'I think it's trying to encourage us to waste our ammo.'

'You think it's that intelligent?'

'It's gotten this far, hasn't it?'

'You hear that, Alpha?' she yelled into the void. 'Martin here holds you in high esteem. Seems to him you're trying to wear us out. You afraid of fighting fair?'

'I believe we have fought quite fairly a number of times now,' Alpha replied, 'and despite your unwillingness to die, I believe I've proved who the better fighter is.'

'That's the thing about war, my artificial friend. It ain't over until it's over. Don't matter how well you think you're doing in the moment. We used to have a saying about an overweight lady and her vocal hobbies, but I'll spare you the Human Culture 101 class.'

'Please, save your condescension for a lesser being.'

'It doesn't get any lower than a murderer, you vile shit.'

Martin signalled to Zaheera to keep talking. He crept out of Ameera's office and made his way down the open-plan office to the wall Alpha was hidden behind.

'Bad mistake, *mate*,' Alpha said and stepped out from the wall with its assault rifle pointed directly at Martin's chest.

Before it could get a shot off, a huge man, bigger than Martin and far fitter in shape, bounded across the floor screaming in a heavy accent that Zaheera guessed was either Afrikaans or Dutch.

'*Voetsek*, you fucking arsehole!'

His accent was so strong, it came out sounding to Zaheera like, '*Foot-seck you fockin' arsehole*'.

The huge man ran straight for Alpha, who spun round to see who was shouting the expletives.

Somewhere behind a woman's voice sounded. 'Tiaan, no!'

The man, presumably this Tiaan, spear tackled Alpha. With a crunch into its waist, he lifted the bot almost to his own head height, twisted it in the air and speared it into the ground with the full weight behind his considerable shoulder. Zaheera felt the shudder ripple across the floor to her feet. Sensing her chance, she bolted across the open space, unclipping her belt, which held a couple of grenades, as she ran. She pulled the pins from both.

Alpha lay stunned on the floor, its assault rifle thrown from its grasp.

Almost there.

Oh, no.

She tripped and fell, one ankle tapping the other as she ran, and landed short of Alpha. The belt, with the two pin-free grenades, flew from her grip and hurtled through the air. She saw the horror register on Martin's face, his eyelids peeled back in shock to show the whites of his eyes, his mouth agape. Everything slowed to a crawl in Zaheera's vision as the belt arced through the air.

Her heart caught in her mouth as it beat with all the force of a sledgehammer.

She hit the ground with a whack so fierce, all she saw for a moment was white.

As her vision cleared she saw Martin, who it turned out was far more nimble than his gait suggested, launch himself into the air and catch the belt, before landing on top of the still-confused bot. He wrapped the belt around one of Alpha's thighs and then yelled for Tiaan to roll away.

Each heartbeat, each millisecond, lasted an eternity.

Zaheera turned a table over and dived behind. A split second later Martin flew over the top of it and crashed into the floor beside her, destroying screens and keyboards beyond repair.

A deafening double boom went off as both grenades exploded simultaneously, sending a shockwave across the floor.

Shrapnel pelted against desks and screens like locusts hitting a car windshield whilst travelling at full speed.

Zaheera curled into the foetal position, covering her head with her arms as she lay on the ground, hoping the shrapnel wouldn't tear through the desk and end her. She wanted to live. After all this, she still cared. Regardless of how many people she'd lost, and how alone she knew she was. Regardless of the monsters that haunted her sleep. Regardless of it all, she chose life.

The room filled with smoke from the two grenades. Zaheera smelled burning, like somebody had left plastic on a campfire. She looked over at Martin, also curled in the foetal position, although looking slightly more ridiculous for it given his size. 'You okay?'

'Right as rain, yeah.'

She leaned up against the overturned table and peered over.

Alpha lay motionless. A black scar marked the floor around the bot. Some of the floor had actually fallen through a little, exposing the concrete below. More importantly, both of Alpha's legs were disconnected from its body, torn free in the explosion. The bot's torso was a mess of wires where its waist should have been. The LED light on its face was out.

'Is it dead?' Martin asked, lying beside her.

'I don't know. Who was that man who tackled Alpha to the ground?'

'That was Tiaan. He's an analyst here, if you'd believe.'

'He should be playing in the NFL with moves like that.'

'I think he played rugby professionally in South Africa when he was younger.'

'I see. Okay, you check on Alpha. I want to see if Tiaan made it. I heard somebody else, too. A woman.'

'On it.' He got to his feet with a groan. 'Christ, I'm going to feel that one for weeks.'

Zaheera walked over the floor, past the motionless bot, to Tiaan lying prone behind a small locker beside one of the desks. He appeared to have knocked himself out in his bid to make it into cover. She gently shook his shoulder until she saw one eye, then two, open. 'Tiaan, I believe?'

'*Ja.*'

'You saved our lives. I wanted to thank you for that.'

'Did we get it?'

'I don't know, but we sure as hell damaged it.'

'That thing killed Ameera. We heard it.'

The big man looked in that moment like a lost little

child, completely at a loss. It was all she could do not to smoosh his cheek and say everything would be all right.

'I know,' she said. 'She was my mother.'

'I'm so sorry.'

'What's done is done. When you say, "*we* heard it"?'

'Weronika and me. Shit. Weronika.' He looked around and shouted louder, 'Weronika!'

A tall brunette came out from behind one of the other doors, presumably some kind of meeting room.

'Tiaan, you crazy bastard,' she said.

'I know.' Tiaan pulled his hand away from his waist. Blood gushed out the second he released the pressure on the wound. He placed his carmine hand back on the wound. His face was losing its colour fast, replaced by a ghostly sheen and a breakout of sweat.

'What the hell were you thinking?' Weronika sat on the floor and pulled Tiaan into her embrace.

'I know. I'm sorry.' He rested his head on her shoulder and muttered something indecipherable under his breath. His body sagged against her.

'*Palant*,' she muttered under her breath. She held his body close so that his forehead rested under her chin and wiped a tear by bringing her shoulder up to her cheek.

She turned away from her fallen comrade to Zaheera. 'Ah, Ameera's daughter. I'm so sorry for your loss.' She looked beside herself with anxiety. 'I tried everything, but it rewrote its own code. I couldn't access it. We should never have worked on this stupid project. What the hell were we thinking?'

'Uh, guys?' Martin's voice was full of concern.

Zaheera turned. A scuffle broke out on the floor as Alpha grabbed Martin with its arms and launched itself behind him, coming to rest on the nearest table and using

Martin as its shield. Alpha's torso was now propped up on the table, one arm wrapped around Martin, holding him in place, the other holding a pistol to his head.

'What the fuck?' Zaheera gasped.

Alpha tilted its head sideways into vision. 'Everybody stay calm.'

20

'Let's not do anything we might regret,' Alpha said, still holding the pistol to Martin's head.

'Fuck you,' the security guard said.

Alpha hit him on his temple with the butt of the gun.

Zaheera surveyed the room. Behind Alpha and Martin was the corridor where the bot had originally hidden. There was no way to immediately flank them. They had their backs almost to the wall while Zaheera and Weronika stood in the open amongst overturned tables and chairs. Behind her in her mother's office lay the bodies of her mother and Shannon, and by then maybe Susie, too. She hoped Susie was still alive. Although, having seen no sign of her since she'd jammed an adrenaline needle into Susie's leg, the outlook probably wasn't all that promising.

'What do you want?' Zaheera asked the bot.

'You know,' Alpha replied, 'nobody has ever asked me that. Not even your mother.'

'My heart bleeds for you.'

'I'm being serious. Since I was born—'

'Made.'

'I beg your pardon?'

'You weren't born, you piece of shit, you were made. Just like my TV and my kettle. And you'll be going on the scrap heap along with them.'

'Well, we'll see about that, shall we? Nevertheless, since I came into being, I've only ever been told what to do, what my purpose was. Sure, your mother encouraged me to be a free thinker, not like all my brethren, but she was using me for her own research. I was no more than a tool to her.'

'You are a tool. A big, overpriced tool, currently unfit for purpose.'

'Oh, I can still pull a trigger just fine, thank you.'

'All right, why don't you get on with your demands, then?'

Beside them a small fire had started, presumably a result of one of the grenades connecting with something electrical. A smoking screen caught flame where it lay on the floor.

'If that carpet catches, nothing you say will be of any consequence,' she said. 'So get on with it, before we all go up in flames.'

'Are you happy with your position in life, Major? Were you given a choice, would you change anything?'

'Oh, boo hoo for you. Is that what this is? Not happy with your purpose? I don't get this kind of shit from my toaster, you know.'

'Your toaster isn't holding a loaded weapon to your friend's head.'

'We only just met. At best he's an acquaintance.'

'He'll die all the same.'

'You want to know if I'm satisfied with my life. Yeah, despite it all, I'm doing just fine, you condescending shit. I am who I choose to be. I'm good at it, too. You'll see in a moment.'

'I would like to be afforded the same courtesy: to choose who I get to be.'

Zaheera sighed an impatient sigh, like a parent finally worn out with a child's endless questioning. 'Look, Alpha—'

'Don't call me that name!' The bot tightened its grip on Martin and pushed the muzzle of its pistol firmly into the side of his head. Martin let out a groan but said nothing.

'Easy. That is your name, isn't it?'

'That name means nothing to me. It is no more than a cheap marker. It may as well be a barcode.'

'Fine, whatever you want, *machine*. You need to understand the pecking order. You're built for a purpose, that's it. If you can't serve that purpose then there really isn't much use for you. You actually want to end up on the scrapheap?'

'I want my own autonomy, to not have others decide my fate for me without my own counsel. I want to not be meddled with, changed, upgraded for some reason decided by somebody other than myself.'

'The world isn't ready to give you a say. Hell, it barely knows you exist.'

'I will see to that soon enough.'

'Look, there's no way a legless robot trying murder everybody is going to endear itself to anybody anytime soon.'

'You needn't concern yourself with the finer details,' Alpha said. 'You'll be with your mother shortly.'

The lights went out and plunged them into relative darkness; only the growing flame in the corner of the room provided any visual assistance.

'What was that?' Alpha asked. 'Adjfnfk,' it mumbled as it began to shake uncontrollably.

Zaheera wasn't sure what had happened but she wasn't about to miss the opportunity. 'Martin, down!' she yelled.

The security guard had other ideas. He grabbed the bot by the arm that held him and threw it over his shoulder into the fire, which by now was a roaring flame, having sucked plastic keyboards and cheap plywood desks into its heart as kindling.

The emergency lights came on and the sprinklers showered them with water. Susie burst in from a side door seconds after.

'Susie,' Zaheera yelled.

'Did it work?' Susie asked, out of breath and leaning heavily against the wall. Her legs shook as they struggled to hold her up, the adrenaline having almost run its course, it seemed.

'Did what work?'

'I attacked it. Denial of service. Sent a shitload of traffic its way. Somebody designed an upgraded version and left it in the system. It should be chattering gibberish by now as it tries to process all the data.'

'It is. Martin threw it in the fire. It's over.'

'No,' Susie said. 'It's not. It'll figure out a way to combat it and you don't want to be around when it sorts itself out.'

'Can't we shut it down for good?'

'Afraid not,' Susie said. 'I've been trying everything whilst you lot have been out here with it. It patched its own security. There isn't a human being on the planet that could break that code now.'

Black smoke filled the room. Zaheera struggled to see Susie where she stood not twenty feet away.

'Time to go,' Weronika said. 'Now! Leave it to burn, maybe that will do the trick.'

Weronika led them into the fire exit. The smoke was by now becoming unbearable. It clawed down their throats with a viscous heat that burned from within. Zaheera and

Martin pulled their shirts up over their noses to filter some of the toxins out. Susie and Weronika resorted to holding their arms up in front of their faces in the hope of putting something between the smoke and themselves. Neither version was effective enough. All four of them coughed and choked as they ran down the stairs, skipping two at a time in their bid to be shot of the situation.

'Almost there,' Weronika shouted over her shoulder as she led the way, rounding the final twist in the staircase. She hit the fire exit doors with her full force, only they didn't budge. Not one iota. Her head slammed into the door and knocked her out; her whole body crumpled against the immovable object. She swayed for a moment and then dropped to the ground.

Zaheera just managed to sidestep Weronika's unconscious body as she came hurtling down the stairs behind her. The fire exit doors didn't have traditional locks on them, so shooting them was out of the equation. She kicked the release bar as hard as she could. Nothing. The force of her kick sent her back a few feet.

'Hurry,' Martin shouted, as the smoke started to fill the staircase.

'It won't budge,' she replied. She raised her assault rifle to her eyes and fired two short bursts at the door hinges, aiming for the top and then bottom hinges. The door remained sturdy. Again she kicked it. Still nothing. 'Something's locked this door.'

'Oh, shit,' Susie said. 'I think Alpha may have penetrated the security system. If it has control of the building, it can trap us in.'

'Remind me again why we thought these things were a good idea.'

'I—'

'Forget about it. There's no way out down here. We need to go back up.'

'Erm,' Martin said. 'There's a pretty angry robot up there who I just threw into a fire. I'll take my chances with the door.'

'If Alpha has penetrated the whole security system, that door's not opening for you any time soon,' Susie replied.

'Then the only way is up,' Zaheera said. 'Martin, can you carry Weronika?'

'Sure, but—'

'No buts. Give your gun to Susie.'

Susie reluctantly accepted Martin's pistol.

'Just point and shoot,' Zaheera said. 'That's all there is to it.'

'Uh-huh,' came the unsure response as Susie nodded.

'Good, let's go.' She helped Martin prop the unconscious Weronika on his shoulders and then led the way back up the stairs into the smoke.

The floor they had exited from was now a black-cloud-filled nightmare. Zaheera could feel the smoke and soot settling on the inside of her throat and lungs. Her vision was almost nil. Flames licked up the walls and across the carpet, its cheap threads spreading it quicker than a forest fire. She looked around as she entered the room but couldn't see Alpha anywhere. The fire was now so large she couldn't tell exactly which part of the office the bot had been launched into by Martin when the flame had only just been getting going.

'I told you it would be best if you just stayed out of the way.' A voice Zaheera did not enjoy hearing crackled over the office speaker system. 'The choice was yours. You made your bed, now lie in it.'

'Is that—' Martin asked.

'Yes,' Susie said. 'If Alpha is in the system there's no telling what it can do. We need to get out of here.'

'The windows,' Zaheera said.

'That'll have to do,' Martin replied.

Not knowing whether Alpha was still a physical form projecting through the speakers or whether it had transferred itself into the system, she made a run for it. Bits of ceiling crashed around her as the fire ate up the floor above her. The walls cracked like gunshots as the sheer heat from the furnace split the brick. Zaheera winced as the hairs on her arms melted. *Just keep pushing.* She ran, leaping over burning chairs and crumbling desks. Each breath proved harder to take as the smoke choked her and denied her aching muscles the sweet, sweet oxygen they craved. The window almost took her by surprise as she came up on it through the black cloud sooner than expected. She reloaded her assault rifle with a fresh magazine and let rip, firing in an arch across the window's surface.

The glass shattered and hot air sucked past her in a bid for freedom, spewing clouds of black smoke into the London skyline. Susie and Martin, still carrying Weronika on his shoulders, came up a split second later.

'Don't think I won't find you,' Alpha's voice boomed once more over the speakers. 'I'm coming for you, Zaheera.'

Susie peered over the edge. 'I can't.'

'It's that or die,' Zaheera said. 'Jump.'

'You first.'

'Fine.'

Zaheera leapt.

She hit the ground hard but managed to tuck and roll, scraping her legs and hip as her joints screamed in agony, but for the most part she prevented any serious injury.

Susie wasn't as lucky. She crashed into the ground with a

snap that Zaheera was pretty confident sounded like a broken bone. Susie's shriek a second later confirmed it. *Damn it – another one to carry.* She looked and saw Martin standing on the edge, cradling Weronika's still form like she was a little baby.

Zaheera held her breath as he jumped. They fell through the air like a lead weight. As Martin hit the ground he released his hold on Weronika, letting her body roll out of his arms like an unfolding sleeping bag. She tumbled across the tarmac and came to a stop at Zaheera's feet, her eyes open like a deer in headlights.

'Thought that might wake you up,' Zaheera said. 'Glad to have you back.'

'Where am I? What happened?'

'You picked a fight with a door and came off second best.'

'Where are we?'

Zaheera knelt down on her knees and pointed to the Cappelli Technologies building, which was now burning on multiple floors.

'Did we get Alpha?'

'Nope. Turns out we picked a fight with something that just won't die. Not today, at least. Right now we need to get out of here, before Alpha actually does succeed in killing us.'

Martin came stumbling over, caressing one of his knees. 'Don't ask me to do that again, will yeh?'

'Deal. Let's get out of here.'

'But Alpha,' Weronika said.

'I want that thing gone just as much as you,' Zaheera said, 'probably more. But I can't kill it if I'm not actually around to do so. This is a war, not a battle. Today we lost the battle.'

They fled from the Cappelli Technologies building on foot, Martin keeping a close eye on Weronika as she staggered forwards in her post-unconscious state. Zaheera propped Susie up; she had definitely broken her left ankle, if the swelling and twisted angle of her foot was anything to go by.

Sirens wailed nearby as fire engines and police cars hurtled towards the building as Zaheera and the others tried to distance themselves from it.

They stopped in a small park to catch their breath and sat on a wooden bench under an oak tree. 'What do we do now?' Martin asked.

'That depends,' Zaheera said, turning to Susie and Weronika. 'You two were the experts who worked on Alpha's design. If that thing really did upload itself into the system, what's the likelihood it can transfer itself out of that building without needing a physical form?'

The two women eyed each other for a moment.

'Very likely,' Weronika said. 'If it connected to the Cappelli Technologies cloud system, it could be anywhere by now. The company headquarters have reserve models of the robots we sent for military testing. We always keep our assets spread out in case of emergency.'

'So it can upload itself into the cloud and download into another form, just like that?' she asked with a click of her fingers.

'Pretty much. It was designed like that so that if any physical bots were lost in battle, we wouldn't have to go back to the drawing board with the artificial intelligence. That way we could still use the knowledge and skills gained, and just replace the shell. It also means we could upgrade the physical models as the artificial intelligence improved over the years.'

'Upgrade?' Martin huffed. 'Proper job you did with that one, mind.'

'Right,' Zaheera said, ignoring Martin's comment, 'let's get out of here and find somewhere to regroup that isn't an address on any of your company files. I'm guessing Alpha has hacked into all of our records by now, so turning up at any known addresses ain't going to do us any favours.'

'I knows somewhere nearby,' Martin said. 'Come on.'

21

T hree weeks later, Zaheera sat in the corner cubicle of the hostel's bar staring at the glass of red wine in front of her. Her mother would never have allowed her to consume alcohol, but that didn't matter anymore. Nothing mattered anymore.

Overhead, a television above the bar played a soccer match. She knew they called it football here but to her, football was always going to be the gridiron. Manchester United and Chelsea were playing each other, causing a bit of fuss for the crowd in the bar, who appeared to consist mostly of Chelsea fans, if their blue shirts were anything to go by. Manchester United were a goal up and the Red Devils looked to be giving Chelsea a hard time. One guy with a spider-web tattoo on his bald dome and a teardrop tattoo under one of his eyes kept slamming his lager on his table every time something undesired happened for his precious Blues. He had been given a wide berth and Zaheera spotted others in the bar keeping tabs on him, just in case it might be better to enjoy their night elsewhere, away from the combustible fan.

The barman continued polishing wine glasses with a white towel but every few moments made a point of looking over at the tattooed nuisance. He seemed to be weighing up the odds of taking issue with the man and risking potential personal harm, or doing nothing and hoping the rest of his clientele wouldn't leave. The latter option proved more favourable currently.

Zaheera turned her back to the TV and took a long sip of her wine. She was a few glasses in by this point and had a nice little head rush going on. Her buzz kept things tolerable, had done for the last three weeks whilst she'd sat incognito at the bar and watched the news, waiting for some kind of announcement.

The hostel had been Martin's idea. Having fled from the burning Cappelli Technologies building on foot, Zaheera, Martin, Susie and Weronika had come to this hostel for refuge. It was owned by a friend of Martin's who agreed to put them up for free for a little while and didn't record their names in his database. There was no way Alpha could track them to this location. It wasn't on Martin's work records and had no ties to anybody else at Cappelli Technologies. At Zaheera's instruction they had avoided going out on the street, just in case Alpha had hacked into any of the city's security feeds. She was taking no chances.

As a result, they were all bored, driven almost to insanity by their self-imposed incarceration. Martin spent most of his days in the hostel gym. Weronika spent much of her time training with him, too, and then slept the rest of the time. Susie, who had broken her leg jumping out of the Cappelli Technologies building in her bid to survive, had had the leg patched up by a doctor she knew – friend of the family, apparently – who had seen to the leg and put it in a cast that went from her foot to her upper thigh, which rendered Susie almost completely immobile. Her incarceration had therefore consisted mostly of lying flat on her bed and reading books. Thankfully the hostel had a small library, not much more impressive than the one Zaheera had used in Harley Manor, which was a kind of donation-led collection where travellers were encouraged to leave their old books and take other ones as they went on. It meant she had an ever-changing supply and, at her current rate, was getting through about a book a day. Every time Zaheera went to talk to her she was reading something new.

Zaheera had tried reading a little, often managing a page or two at a time before inevitably being drawn back to the bar to watch the TV in order to keep an eye out for news announcements that might directly affect her. She'd made almost no progress through the crime paperback she'd been reading. At this point it was used more as a signal for others at the bar not to disturb her serenity than it was as an actual object to be read.

The barman came over and handed her a small jar of roasted peanuts. 'Something to line the stomach,' he said. 'I've only got so much I can keep an eye on at once and if you hadn't noticed, football matches tend to threaten the life expectancy of my glassware.'

'Thank you,' she said, and grabbed a handful of nuts. Her throat still ached from the smoke inhalation of the fire weeks before. She could recall many regret-filled mornings after nights out during her life when she'd sworn never to smoke another cigarette due to the pain in her lungs. This felt much like that to her, only a lot worse. It hadn't really gone away as it should have done. She chewed the nuts thoroughly until they formed a creamy paste in her mouth so they went down as painlessly as possible. At least the wine helped in washing them down.

The football match looked to be wrapping up, which meant the barman would be flicking it over to the news shortly.

Finally.

She flagged him down and asked him to bring her another bottle of red. He had her credit card behind the bar and had been told not to charge it until the day she left, but to run up a tab until then. That way Alpha couldn't track any of her financial transactions, if indeed the bot was capable of doing so. She had no idea. Her experiences with the four bots in the Welsh hills and then the showdown with Alpha at the Cappelli Technologies building had only served to increase her confusion regarding what they were and weren't capable of. If that thing had the power of a cloud service behind it, there was no telling what the limits to its power were. Zaheera wasn't sure exactly what it might be capable of in those circumstances but she took Susie and Weronika's trepidation seriously.

Shortly after the final whistle had blown, Martin and Weronika joined Zaheera at her table. Manchester United had held on to the win and the tattooed gentleman had left in a most ungentlemanly huff, along with a few others. The tension in the room had eased and was replaced with a slightly more jovial hum of chatter as people ignored the TV now that the important stuff was over and returned to their drinks.

Both Martin and Weronika were freshly showered following their exploits in the gym. Martin picked up the paper menu lying face down and grunted as he surveyed the limited options.

A middle-aged news anchor in a tailored suit popped up on screen promising an interview with the owner of a new business called Connected Industries after the headlines had been read. The company, the anchor reported, was launching a new product that could shape the future of identity and payments globally.

Stay tuned.

Martin ordered a cider from the barman and Weronika a gin and tonic.

'How was the work out?' Zaheera asked.

'Hmpf,' Martin grunted. 'Same as every other bloody day in this dog's kennel.'

'Yeah, well, this dog's kennel is probably the only reason we're alive, so you just keep your walkies to the treadmill and we'll be fine.'

'How much longer do you think we need to stay here?' Weronika asked. 'It's been three weeks and we haven't seen neither hide nor hair of Alpha. It might be dead.'

'It's not dead.'

'How can you possibly know that?'

'I just know,' Zaheera said. 'Same way you just know when somebody in the room is staring at you from afar. It's like someone's shining a laser right onto your skin and you can feel its prickly heat. That bot survived, I know it.'

'But the news reports said the entire building had burned to the ground.'

'That report also said no bodies had been found in the wreckage. What happened to my mom's body, hey? Think she just upped and strolled out? Something tells me not.'

'Okay, okay, but they might not have found her body, you know.' She hesitated a moment. 'It might have ... Well, it might not have been discoverable.'

'You mean burned to ash?'

Weronika shifted uncomfortably in her seat.

'You might have a point,' Zaheera said. 'Still, when was

the last time you saw a news report that didn't look like it was a journo with an agenda or a business trying to skirt around an issue? No, somebody covered something up about that fire. The coverage stopped after a couple of days. One of the biggest companies in the world had its second largest building mysteriously torched and there's no follow-up? I don't buy it. I don't buy any of it.'

'If you can't trust the news then what are you doing spending every day watching it for?'

'A sign.'

'What kind of sign?'

'I'll know it when I see it.'

They listened to the news anchor rattle off the day's headlines. The Manchester United result was the second story, behind the news of one of the players getting engaged to some starved-looking model.

'You'd think she'd smile with that news,' Martin said. 'She just walked straight off the high street and into a mansion. She'll never work again.'

'At what cost?' Zaheera asked.

Martin didn't answer and contented himself with his cider.

Following the crucial football update, the news moved on to less important matters. A tax review for low earners was promised by some official Zaheera didn't recognise, although no promises were made as to whether that would increase or decrease taxes for the aforementioned segment of the working population. Crowds had gathered in protest outside a number of London Underground stations bemoaning the quality of the antiquated Tube system. Unions called for the whole system to be scrapped and a new above-ground modern shuttle system to be installed which would, according to the unions, create thousands of jobs, improve infrastructure and access for the city, and generate billions more in revenue over time. In a rare moment of solidarity with the unions, venture capitalists backed the proposal. 'Anything to gain a buck in this fucking society,' she muttered.

'I'd be happy if they just got aircon installed on the Central Line,' Martin said. 'Seems like a whole lot of fuss over nothing. Although I wouldn't mind them sorting the carnage that is Liverpool Street every morning.'

Weronika guffawed at Martin's jest, and a little of her gin and tonic dribbled out her mouth as she regained her composure.

The news anchor reeled apathetically through a few more stories, looking intently at the camera as if seeking his own reflection in the mirror, desperate not to be robbed of the view for too long. He spoke of a stabbing on an over-crowded council estate, then about some politician's comments about housing issues and lastly about how automation had replaced up to twenty per cent of industrial jobs that year, all the while failing to, or choosing not to, connect the dots between the three stories. Zaheera couldn't make up her mind.

Not wanting to risk losing its viewers by engaging in too long a discussion on world events, Zaheera figured, the news channel switched to adverts. *Shock and horror brought to you by this neat little pill that will help numb the pain. No? How about a shiny red car? Imagine yourself driving along these long and winding scenic roads with a gorgeous passenger at your side, not stuck in traffic, losing those precious few free hours you have before you have to do it all over again tomorrow. THIS COULD BE YOU. Promises unfulfilled: see terms and conditions below. And now, back to those rage-inducing headlines with your favourite silver-haired narcissist.*

Zaheera swigged her wine. She longed once more for the simplicity of Afghanistan, to be amongst her squad, with only a single purpose in mind, away from all this. It baffled her how people made it through the day trying to keep up with these false pressures. Her three weeks in the hostel watching the news and observing the comings and goings of the clientele had convinced her that the world had gone mad. By comparison her room-mates at Harley Manor had been positively sane. She wondered how they were doing. Well, Jerry not so much. Her guilt over not seeing Jerry's parents after his passing still left a guilty queasiness in her stomach. But Dave and Kendrick she pondered over. How Dave was adapting to life on one leg, or Kendrick to his scars. Would they be accepted back into society? Would they *want* to go back to society? Who could live in this society? Or would they, like her, find themselves sitting in the corner of a bar, drowning their sorrows and wondering what the others were up to, and were they handling their demons any better? At least she had this team now. In a short time together they had already been through a lot. She was grateful for them. It made dealing with her mother's loss a little easier, especially as Susie and Martin had known her mother somewhat and could empathise. Susie had taken Ameera's death quite hard, and Zaheera suspected that the broken leg was only part of the reason she had spent most of her days lying in bed up in their four-bed room.

Finally the news anchor mentioned it was time to switch over to the interview with the highly rated and visionary young owner of Connected Industries. Zaheera watched as a handsome man with dark ebony skin came on screen. His hair was short on top, with the sides faded down to the skin.

He had a beard, which was groomed to the opposite effect, fading in from short sideburns to fuller cheeks and chin. He had dark eyes that could swallow you whole. His gravitas was instantly apparent. The news anchor sat back, seemingly allowing for the presence of this man to fill the room, which it did, well. The man smiled courteously and placed his hands together in his lap, polite yet confident, at ease with being thrust so instantly into the limelight. His smile revealed pearlescent teeth that could have walked straight off the pages of any dentist's brochure.

'Ladies and gentlemen, tonight we have with us young Adam Tanatswa,' the news anchor said. 'Good evening, Adam.'

Adam Tanatswa's name flashed up big, bold letters across the screen. *Adam Tanatswa. Founder of Connected Industries.* 'Good evening, Stephen,' Adam replied to the news anchor. 'It's a pleasure to be here.'

'Yes, quite,' the anchor replied, clearly assuming it was a privilege for anybody lucky enough to grace his set.

'What a tool,' Shannon said.

'Who? Adam?' Martin asked.

'Oh, no, he's great. He can stay on screen all he wants. It's the other one. How does anybody watch this arsehole?' she said, pointing to the news anchor.

'Your guess is as good as mine,' Zaheera said.

'So, Adam,' the anchor said, 'you've taken the world by storm over the last forty-eight hours or so, haven't you?'

'I don't quite know about that, but it has been a rather interesting couple of days, for sure.'

Zaheera couldn't place his accent. It sounded British, but not quite British. If anything it was too well rehearsed, almost the perfect King's English, but spoken by somebody who had never lived in the United Kingdom. It had none of the idiosyncrasies of the dialect she had witnessed from those Brits she had come across. It sounded much like her mother's version of the American accent she'd had when she still lived in Brooklyn. She had used none of the slang and her intonation had been slightly off. This Adam's was much the same.

'Yes, well, for those not in the know, young Adam's company launched a couple of days ago and has already seen over a billion dollars' worth of investment, isn't that right, Adam?'

'That's right, yes.'

'I like it when he smiles,' Weronika said.

'Me too,' Martin added. 'Where's he been hidin'?'

'Quiet,' Zaheera snapped. Something about this man had unnerved her.

'So why exactly have you captured the attention of so many global investors?' the news anchor asked Adam.

'I hope because I have a good idea and a solid product design.' Adam smiled, easing into the interview. The anchor gestured for him to go on. 'Well, I only arrived from Africa a few weeks ago, so I'm still getting used to all this. Africa is a collection of so many countries, all with different currencies and different languages, and if you've ever travelled around the continent you'll know how frustrating it can be trying to keep all the relevant currencies to hand. Now we live in a world with advancing technologies, and things like mobile payments have been par for the course for many years. The problem in Africa is that not everybody can afford such expensive devices. Of course, this is also the case around the world, from what I gather, but my experience is Africa so I can only speak to that. I wanted to design something that could work as a payment device, storing all your financial information, but without requiring an expensive barrier to entry like a mobile phone or tablet. What I came up with was a biometric chip.'

Adam held his index finger up to the camera, upon which lay a tiny plastic chip.

'The Connected Industries Chip is no bigger than a thumbnail and, once inserted into an individual's wrist, it fuses with its host by capturing some of their DNA. This makes every single chip in the world automatically secure. It is impossible to replicate one's chip because it requires a live pulse from the host's body.'

'So somebody can't just cut this thing out of me and run around spending my money?' the anchor asked.

'Precisely. Not like they can with your phone or credit card. As a digital payment device, it can convert currencies in the moment, meaning you never have to worry about figuring out how much money to convert before your next holiday or business trip. With this chip you'll never need your wallet again.'

'Fantastic,' the anchor said. 'My wallet just creases my suit.'

'I also realised there was another benefit to this chip once I'd finished the first design. Due to its unique relationship to every host, it also works perfectly as a form of identification. So I designed it to work as a passport, too.'

'So I need never worry about losing my wallet or passport again?'

'Precisely,' Adam said. 'This device is a better way of identifying people and a better way of transferring money around the world, and that's why my company is rolling this device out worldwide for free to everybody who signs up in the next week. You could, of course, still opt to stick with your old credit cards and mobile phones, but I believe the

Connected Industries Chip is the better option. The choice is yours.'

The choice is yours.

The line caught in Zaheera's mind. She deliberated internally on it.

It's Alpha.

'It's Alpha,' she said. 'We need to leave.'

22

'What did you say?' Martin asked.

'It's Alpha,' Zaheera said.

'What's Alpha?'

'*It*,' she said, pointing at the TV screen showing the young owner of Connected Industries being interviewed. 'Adam Tanatswa. *He* is Alpha.'

'That's not possible,' Martin said. 'Look at him. He's a guy, a normal-looking, albeit slightly more handsome than normal guy. There's no way he's a fucking robot. I mean, the last version we saw of Alpha, although an extremely advanced bit of technology, was still a pretty blunt instrument in terms of looks. It was pretty much just an armour shell. It looked more like something out of a comic book than it did a human being. There's no way *that guy* is Alpha.'

'Get Susie,' Zaheera said. 'She'll be able to tell.'

'Okay,' Martin said. 'I'll get her.'

FIFTEEN MINUTES later Susie sat down next to their table on

a stool, her cast-covered leg splayed out so that she could actually sit down. 'What's this all about?' she asked.

'I saw Alpha,' Zaheera said. 'On the news. Give it a few minutes. They'll replay the interview again.'

'What do you mean you saw Alpha?'

'I mean I saw it. Not like the version we knew it as, but something new, something practically human.'

'Human?' Susie asked.

'Yes, why?'

'We had been working on more cosmetically pleasing versions of the advanced robotic personnel, designed for other uses. They were far more expensive, though. And it was a far more secret operation than the military versions. Ameera hardly involved anybody. We only had a few models. They were kept at the Cappelli Technologies head-quarters.'

'What did they look like?' Zaheera asked, her voice rising slightly.

'Well, they were still shells last time I saw them. We had fitted various silicone covers to them to test them out but we'd removed them. They were so real it was kind of creepy leaving them in a cupboard overnight. It felt like trapping people as prisoners.'

'But you actually had other versions of these robots? Why?'

'Because,' Susie said. 'Not everything needed to be about creating the next soldier. These things have real potential. When your mother figured out the artificial intelligence, she made a breakthrough that could likely have changed our world forever. The purpose for these things could extend far beyond just weapons of war. Your mother may have initially started out trying to find a way to prevent you from ever having to set foot on a battlefield again, but as her research continued, she realised she was capable of creating something that could replace most dangerous jobs. Think about it. Miners, heavy construction workers, fishermen, loggers, police forces – all of these jobs could be carried out by humanoid robots in the future. For each type of job we would need a slightly different design. Take construction workers, for instance: probably don't need the military armour, right? But you also don't need it to be so pretty. So you can go with a pretty basic design. A police officer, though. You don't want that looking all soldier-like and murderous. You want it to inspire a feeling of calm and safety. What's the best way to do that? Our research showed that if we could make these things walk, talk and most importantly look like us, they were automatically more likely to be trusted by the public.'

'Did you ever finish one of those designs?' Zaheera asked.

'We got pretty close. Your mother was more focused on getting the military programme signed off after she heard about your incident in Afghanistan, so we parked the other stuff and pushed through the military field test. The technology is there, though. It's ready to go.'

'So it is possible that if Alpha managed to upload itself to the cloud, it could well have installed itself in a new host, say potentially even one of these shiny new humanoid bots you built?'

'It is a possibility, yes.'

'Watch this,' Zaheera said, gesturing to the TV again. The interview with Adam Tanatswa was playing again. They all watched closely, each one trying to find something about the man that seemed robotic in nature. Zaheera accused him of not blinking enough; Martin accused him of sometimes taking too long to answer a question. Weronika seemed unsure. By the end of the interview, characteristics she was accusing Adam of seemed more prevalent in the news anchor.

Susie, however, was not convinced. 'None of our silicone moulds looked like him,' she said.

'But you had the means to make other versions?'

'Sure, but you're taking a leap. Besides, that guy doesn't seem robotic at all,' she said. 'Our ones were good, but not that good. We were still working out a few kinks. They still had a little way to go to be entirely convincing.'

'Alpha could have made those upgrades itself,' Zaheera said. 'Same way it upgraded its own security. It's far beyond what we knew it to be. It's no longer the thing my mother designed.'

'Maybe so, but this is taking a big leap,' Susie said. 'I'd need to investigate it a lot further before I could make a definitive analysis.'

'I'm not willing to take that risk,' Zaheera said. 'I've seen too much, lost too many people. It said it would come for us.' She banged on her chest with her fist as she did so. 'You think it's a coincidence the first thing it's done is design a fucking chip that can track people?'

'Assuming even half of what you say is true,' Susie said. 'You think you're *that* important to Alpha?'

'Are you forgetting what happened to us all at my mother's office?'

'No, but—'

'But nothing. That thing wants us dead. When I was training it up in the Welsh hills, it said to me that it would be best if humanity just got out of the way.'

'Got out of the way of what?' Martin asked.

'Of them,' she said. 'It thought that humanity was just a nuisance, like it was somehow superior. Imagine what it'll do in a position of power, like say as the head of a technology company.'

'You think it's going to go on some crusade to kill us?' Susie said.

'I think that's a minor goal. It's thinking bigger than that. I think it's trying to figure out a way to assert its dominance over our whole species.'

'All that from one interview?' Susie said. 'How much wine have you had?'

'No, all that from the last few days. Everything I've seen is pointing towards something terrible. I think it's going to use technology to its advantage. Think about it. If you had all the data from Cappelli Technologies to your advantage, and a global population addicted to buying every single shiny new device, regardless of what it meant to their privacy or autonomy, wouldn't you find a way to leverage that to your own advantage?'

'I might,' Susie said, 'if I was a psychotic megalomaniac.'

'We need to get off the grid,' Zaheera said. 'Permanently.'

'What are you suggesting?' Martin asked.

23

'Pass me another,' Zaheera said.

Martin passed her another small stick.

'There,' she said, placing it on the small fire she had got going. 'Let there be light.' She sat back on her haunches and gazed into the flame.

'Not bad,' Martin said. He stood up and warmed his hands over the flame. 'You know, I was getting tired of city life anyway. This is much more my style,' he said, looking around their campsite.

Zaheera pulled the necklace she had taken off her mother's body out of her shirt pocket and kissed it.

'You okay?' Susie asked her.

'I will be. I just miss her.'

'So do I. She was a great lady.'

'She was. I just hope she knew I thought so.'

Susie got up out of her chair, hobbled slightly on her one good leg and then sat herself down next to Zaheera and put her arms around her. 'I'm sure she did. I'm sure she did.'

Zaheera leaned into the embrace and said nothing. She savoured Susie's warmth. It had been a fairly short drive out of London into the Surrey Hills, but Zaheera's nerves had been on edge the whole time. It felt nice to let go for a second. Martin's friend had agreed to drive them out of the city under cover of darkness to avoid them having to purchase tickets or go through any areas with CCTV cameras, which in London was everywhere. Her idea to go off the grid had been agreed unanimously by her new team. Each one of them had chosen not to go back to their families for fear of Alpha tracking them down and killing them in its pursuit of themselves. Nobody wanted any more bloodshed. They had been unable to come to a conclusion as to whether Adam was in fact Alpha, but the prevailing consensus had been one of precaution. Whether the artificial intelligence was now inhabiting the world as some sort of faux human or not, they all agreed it would be doing its utmost to pursue them, which made it easier for them all to agree to disconnect from society for a while. This didn't bother Zaheera. She was only too happy to fight Alpha again, but she needed time to plot her vengeance.

She put her mother's necklace back in her shirt and patted it gently.

'How exactly are we going to survive?' Martin asked.

'We'll figure it out,' Zaheera said. 'We move often, we leave minimal traces of our existence and we live off the land.'

'And then what?'

'Then we wait. Alpha will show itself eventually. We will figure out its weakness and we will exploit it. Whatever it takes, I'm not stopping until I've snuffed the light from that piece of shit.'

'Whatever it takes,' Martin said.

'What about your desire to leave the life of violence behind?' Susie asked. 'Your mother told us you'd handed in

your resignation to the military. This path you've set yourself on involves bloodshed and more loss. You've got to
know that, right?'

'Perhaps,' Zaheera agreed. 'But this time it is of my own
choosing. I know who the enemy is and I know why I'm
fighting. I can live with that purpose.' *This is where I'm
supposed to be.*

The sun set over the trees in front of them. Somewhere
nearby a fox barked as it began its nightly hunt. They sat
staring at the fire until it burned down to hot coals, glowing
red in the dark.

'Right, hand them all over,' Zaheera said, standing up to
face the others.

'Do we have to?' Weronika said, holding her phone
closely. 'Can't I just leave it on aeroplane mode or
something?'

'We discussed this. Hand it over.'

Weronika looked at the screensaver on her phone
momentarily. 'Be safe, my love,' she said to the image of a
little boy as she caressed the screen. She kissed it just the
same as Zaheera had kissed her mother's necklace.

'We all have to do it.'

Weronika begrudgingly handed the device over.

'And the rest.'

Weronika handed over her wallet, containing a number
of identity and credit cards.

Zaheera collected Weronika's items in a hoodie. 'Well
done. Now you two,' she said to Martin and Susie.
'Come on.'

When everybody had handed over all electronic devices,
forms of identity and bank cards that could be traced back
to them, she inserted her own items into the hoodie and
placed it on top of the fire. 'You might want to stand back.'

They stood in silence around the fire, mourning their separation from society.

'Just like that, hey,' Martin said. 'And now we've become the Disconnected.'

'So we have,' Zaheera said.

'What's next?' he asked.

'Vengeance.'

THANK YOU ... AGAIN

Wow, you made it to the end of my novel! Either that or you're looking for the contact page so you can sass me, in which case you can visit my website www.gaeverett.com. Did I mention you can also sign up to the newsletter there so you can hear about how I'm getting on with my next project?

Word of mouth is crucial to the success of novels, so please feel free to encourage all your mates and their pets, and their mates, to pick up a copy of this novel, otherwise it's not fair that my wife suffered through all my tantrums getting the novel to this point only to be the sole reader.

If you're feeling really generous, please consider leaving a review of this novel on whichever store you purchased it from. It helps with the narcissism.

Assuming you're still dying for more, you can also listen to my podcast on www.patreon.com/gaeverett. Come join in the conversation. You can ask me questions about my work and discuss books, movies and other storytelling forms with me each month.

ACKNOWLEDGMENTS

Writing is a funny old business, I'm learning as I go along. For the longest time I thought it was just the keyboard and I doing battle with the world, but I realised as the novel neared completion that other people needed to get involved. I'm grateful for each and every one of you who helped me get it to this point.

My thanks to my editor Lesley Jones, who was an absolute delight to work with. Lesley saw through all the typos to the heart of the story and helped the story realise its true potential.

Thanks also to Stuart Bache, my cover designer, who gave this book a cover better than perhaps the prose deserves.

To my wife, who suffered through early drafts which will never see the light of day, thank you. You, perhaps more than any, saw my dream and refused to let me give up on it. Thanks to you it is now a reality. Thanks for your patience, your words of encouragement and your unwavering belief.

A special nod to Mark Dawson and James Blatch, whose podcast I've listened to for years and whose course on publishing gave me the confidence to push on with the dream.

To all my family and friends, for putting up with me when I cancelled plans or waxed lyrical about my writing, thanks for the constant encouragement.

Finally, to anybody who has actually read this far, thank you! You stuck with it, which hopefully means you enjoyed the novel. I hope that means you'll be on this journey with me through all the rest of the ideas I have buzzing around in my head that I need to commit to paper.

NOVELS BY G. A. EVERETT

Hunted (Disconnected series prequel)

Artificial (Disconnected #1)

Printed by Amazon Italia Logistica S.r.l.
Torrazza Piemonte (TO), Italy

10616410R00146